"Why don't we have a good time together?"

Holt smiled lazily. "We both know the score. I'm not ready for marriage, but it might be amusing to play a little trick on my mother, and really it would serve her right."

Avis burst out indignantly, "I'm not sure I know what you mean by 'having a good time,' but I certainly wouldn't agree to giving your mother the impression that we'd—we'd fallen for each other at first sight. I happen to like her, and you don't deceive people you like."

They had arrived back at the house now, and Holt stopped the car. He said with a grin, "Couldn't it be true, lovely Avis? Don't you believe in love at first sight?"

Books by Marjorie Lewty

HARLEQUIN ROMANCES

HARLEQUIN PRESENTS

These books may be available at your local bookseller.

For a list of all titles currently available, send your name and address to:

Harlequin Reader Service
P.O. Box 52040, Phoenix, AZ 85072-2040
Canadian address: P.O. Box 2800, Postal Station A,
5170 Yonge St., Willowdale, Ont. M2N 5T5

Riviera Romance

Marjorie Lewty

Harlequin Books

TORONTO • NEW YORK • LONDON
AMSTERDAM • PARIS • SYDNEY • HAMBURG
STOCKHOLM • ATHENS • TOKYO • MILAN

Original hardcover edition published in 1984
by Mills & Boon Limited

ISBN 0-373-02650-1

Harlequin Romance first edition October 1984

CHAPTER ONE

Avis's first thought was, 'Oh dear, Robert is going to hit the ceiling when I tell him about this!' Her second thought, as she glanced out of the office window at the sleety February rain slanting across the rooftops of the shops opposite and dripping in sodden blobs from the gutters, was, 'A week in the sun—how absolutely marvellous!' Usually this North London residential suburb was a pleasant enough place in which to live and work, but today it wasn't at its most inviting, and the French Riviera sounded like a good exchange.

Mr Hanworthy, senior partner in the solicitors' firm of Hanworthy, Hanworthy and Judd, took off his spectacles and polished them, peering benevolently across the desk at his pretty young secretary, who was sitting with her notebook balanced on her knee, her sherry-coloured eyes glinting, as they always did when she was excited. 'Well, how does it grab you, Avis? A week on the Côte d'Azur, all expenses paid? It sounds to me like a piece of cake.' Mr Hanworthy had a habit of coming out with slang expressions from last year or the year before—though not, of course, in the presence of his clients. Avis found it rather endearing.

'It sounds wonderful. But did Mrs Clavell really ask for me specially?' Avis's forehead wrinkled puzzledly below the mass of silky brown hair.

'Really and truly, cross my heart.' Mr Hanworthy replaced his glasses and picked up a letter from the top of the pile on his desk. 'This is what she says: "I have just seen my doctor and I must have all my papers immediately. I do not trust the post in this place and I think it would be better for you to send someone down to me. I need everything—investments, trust deeds, my will, etc. etc. You will know what to send, dear Mr Hanworthy, and I think you will understand why I am asking for them so urgently." '

Mr Hanworthy raised his eyes from the letter, adding drily, 'Here the good lady puts three exclamation marks, which means, I imagine, that the doctor has probably told her she must take it easy—from which she infers that her decease is imminent. This has happened regularly for several years now, but I must say that every time she visits me, when she's in England, she has always seemed extremely—er—chirpy.'

He read from the letter again. ' "Would you send down that nice girl who works in your office? I think her name was Ava, or something similar. I should want her to stay for a week or so, while I go through everything with my son, who is here at the moment. It would be pleasant to have a pretty face to look at. I am very tired of my elderly bridge parties." ' Mr Hanworthy smiled. 'Another three exclamation marks.' He turned over the page. ' "I am putting myself in your hands—blah blah blah—always so helpful—blah blah—extremely urgent—first possible flight——" ' And so on and so on. She adds a P.S. "I want you to send that girl Ava *most particularly*. *Please* don't send me anyone else." '

He replaced the letter on the desk, smiling, 'You certainly seem to have made a hit with Mrs Clavell, Avis, I really think you must go.' He pulled a wry face. 'We can't afford to lose her goodwill. The lady, as you probably know, is—

er—loaded, and her elder son is a member of our own profession. You may have heard of him—he's with our good friends Denvers, Winterbottom and Bell. He—the son, that is—can't be more than thirty-two or three, but he's a man to be reckoned with already. A formidable counsel——' he stroked his chin '—yes, extremely formidable. Mr Judd is considering briefing him in Smith versus the Mileson Corporation. But that's by the way. Now then, my dear, you have a passport, have you not? When could you be ready to leave?'

Avis hesitated for only a moment. She had a job that she enjoyed and valued and she must be prepared to do what the job demanded of her. Surely Robert wouldn't be unreasonable about that? But she *wasn't* sure. Robert had been very unreasonable about a number of small things recently. Unreasonable and rather inclined to sulk. He wasn't exactly a male chauvinist, but all the same he expected her to be there when he wanted her and to fall in with his plans without argument, and he wasn't nearly so accommodating about falling in with any plans she might make, or even willing to discuss plans jointly.

Avis didn't think of herself as exactly a feminist either, but she considered that men had had it all their own way for a long time, and while she was willing to give and take, the role of doormat didn't appeal to her.

So she smiled across the desk at Mr Hanworthy now and said, 'I could leave any time—tomorrow, if there's a flight. But will you manage all right without me?'

Mr Hanworthy stroked his nose. 'When Mrs Clavell issues an order we lesser mortals must obey,' he said with a whimsical lift of his bushy grey eyebrows. 'I shall make do with Miss

Grimstead and put off everything important until you return to me. Now, run along and see about booking your flight. Come back and tell me what you've managed and we'll telephone through to France to confirm your arrival.'

At one o'clock the Carousel Café in the High Street was crowded, as usual, and thick with cigarette smoke, and today, to make it worse, it was also steamy with wet mackintoshes. Avis and Robert were crushed into a corner, sitting on high stools at the counter, lunching off ham sandwiches and beakers of coffee.

Robert Baines was a sandy-haired, husky young man who worked in the securities department of the local bank. He and Avis played at the same badminton club and had dated regularly through the winter and struck up a habit of meeting at lunchtime at the Carousel, which was handy for both their offices.

Robert, it appeared, had had a bad morning and wasn't in the sweetest of tempers. Predictably then, he received Avis's news peevishly. 'Menton? A week? But you can't possibly go, it's the Bank dinner on Thursday and I want you to come with me.' He took a bite of his ham sandwich and chewed forcibly, as if by doing so he was settling the matter once and for all.

Avis saw trouble brewing, but she kept her voice pleasant. 'Sorry, Robert, I'm afraid I'll have to go. Mr Hanworthy has particularly asked me to.'

The two vertical creases that were beginning to form permanently between Robert's brows became deeper, 'And *I* particularly ask you to come to the dinner with *me*.' The impact of his high-handed statement was rather spoilt as a fat man balancing two plates of egg-and-chips rocked sideways and missed a collision by inches. Robert swore at him and grabbed Avis's arm. 'Let's get out of this—have you finished?'

Avis hadn't finished, but judged it better not to argue, and in any case the atmosphere of the café was getting unbearable. She wrapped the remainder of her sandwiches carefully in a paper napkin, pushed it into her handbag and followed Robert through the crowd.

Outside, the rain was still pouring down. This was, the media reported, the wettest February since records began. They walked together along the streaming pavements, Robert holding his umbrella over the two of them. He was only slightly taller than Avis and she was constantly having to duck and take avoiding action. Robert didn't seem to notice. Having launched on his protest he was pursuing it with vigour. It was, Avis gathered, most thoughtless and selfish of her to agree to go abroad just when his whole future demanded that he should produce her at the Bank dinner.

'You must know how important it is that the directors should know that I'm ready to settle down, and that my wife would be socially acceptable. I'm just coming up to being in line for a sub-managership, and that might tip the scales.'

Avis sloshed along, saying nothing. The cold rain was trickling down her neck and finding its way over the tops of her boots. This was the first time that marriage had been mentioned between them, and it wasn't altogether a surprise, but if Robert thought it was the time and place to discuss it, she just didn't want to know, neither was she flattered by being considered 'socially acceptable'.

They arrived at her office first and she hurried

into the lobby, followed by Robert. He closed his umbrella, after shaking it and depositing another cascade over Avis.

'You do see the point, don't you?' he demanded truculently. 'I'm not making a fuss over nothing, surely you see that?'

She wasn't prepared to argue; all she wanted to do was to get up to the cloakroom and change her wet clothes. 'I'm sorry if you feel I'm letting you down, Robert,' she said, turning towards the lift, 'but I have to do as Mr Hanworthy wants. It's my job.'

Robert stuck out his jaw. 'When we're married you'll give up your job anyway. I wouldn't want my wife to go out to work.'

He really was being rather stuffy; she was finding out a lot about Robert this morning. She had reached the lift now and he had followed her. She put a hand on the gate. 'Look, Robert, I haven't said I'd marry you, you know, because this is the first time you've mentioned it, and I really don't want to stand here, dripping wet, and talk about your career.'

His face went rather pale, his sandy lashes blinked in surprise. 'Avis, you don't mean that! That's not like you.'

She saw that she had amazed and perhaps hurt him, but it couldn't be helped, and he really had been too high-handed altogether. 'We'll talk about it another time—if you still want to talk to me when I come back.' She shook her head at him, smiling, as the lift appeared on the ground floor. 'I *must* go now, Robert, I've got a busy afternoon ahead, getting things straight before I leave.'

She stepped into the lift and pressed the button, and the last thing she saw as she was borne upwards was Robert's astonished face, flushed

with annoyance. She sighed. She hadn't wanted to
hurt him, but really it had been impossible not to,
in the circumstances. If he got over it and saw the
funny side then he would ring her this evening, or
call in at the flat she shared with two other girls. If
not—she shrugged—it would be better to forget
about Robert for good. Just at this moment she
felt so cross with him that it didn't seem to matter
very much.

At eight o'clock that evening, when Avis was
washing her hair and had just reached the
conditioner stage, the bell of the flat rang. Jane
and Janice, her flatmates, were both out, and she
cursed, pulled a cotton top over her jeans,
wrapped a towel round her dripping hair and
padded to the front door. Robert stood there in a
soaking wet raincoat, grinning sheepishly.

'Hullo, Avis.' He looked at her swathed head.
'Have I come at an awkward time?' His tone was
uncharacteristically meek. He parked his dripping
umbrella in the hall outside the door and wiped his
feet carefully.

'That's okay,' she said. 'Sit down while I finish
doing my hair and I'll make us some coffee. I can't
stay long though, I haven't begun to pack yet, and
my flight leaves in the morning early.' Better make
it quite clear from the start that she wasn't going
to be talked out of it.

Talking her out of it was precisely what Robert
had come for, she found, some twenty minutes
later as she sat on the floor in front of the gas-fire,
brushing her silky light-brown hair into its usual
curves round her small, lively face. 'Couldn't you
possibly get out of it?' He sat forward on the sofa,
both hands clasped round his coffee mug. 'Surely
Hanworthy could send someone else—he's got
plenty of girls in the office who could go.

'And Avis,' he hurried on, when she would have spoken, 'I'm sorry I rushed you at lunchtime. I'd sort of taken it for granted that we would get married. I think you're a sweet girl, and it's really time I married now that I'm in line for promotion. I'm sure we'll get on splendidly and make a go of it. So what do you say?' He slid down to the floor beside her. 'Say you will, Avis.' He touched her hair. 'You have such pretty hair,' he murmured. He put his arms round her and drew her towards him and kissed her gently and persuasively.

Robert wasn't the pouncing type. His kisses were pleasant but not overwhelming. If she married Robert she would have a safe life—not very exciting perhaps, but safe. As safe as life can ever be in this uncertain world. Robert would get on in the bank—no doubt about that. She would be a bank manager's wife, with a nice house and garden. And there would be a baby in a pram— two babies—three. Oh, but that would be wonderful; she could almost see the pram under an apple tree in the garden, and a soft, warm glow enveloped her.

Robert drew away and he was smiling. 'Yes?' he queried confidently. 'You'll get out of this trip and come to the Bank dinner with me as my fiancée?'

The picture in Avis's mind had been so beguiling that it was with surprise that she heard herself say, 'No, Robert—I'm sorry, but I've promised and I must go.'

For a moment he stared at her. Then he saw she meant what she said and he got to his feet, straightening his tie. Robert nearly always wore a tie when he wasn't playing badminton. 'Well, I must say I'm surprised. I didn't think you'd let me down.' He walked towards the door and took his raincoat from the back of the chair where he had hung it. 'I take it that my other offer is refused as well,' he said stiffly.

Avis got to her feet, murmuring something trite about remaining friends, but Robert laughed rather nastily. 'I prefer my friends to be loyal,' was his parting shot. 'Goodnight, Avis. I hope you enjoy your holiday!'

He opened the door, retrieved his umbrella and made a dignified exit down the stairs.

Avis sat down weakly. Poor Robert, she had hurt his feelings. Or had she? *Had* Robert very much in the way of feelings? She thought about it for a few moments and decided that the hurt had been more to his pride than anything else. And she needn't feel guilty about the Bank dinner. There was Betty Saunders who had been angling for Robert for some time; she would go with him like a shot if he asked her—which he almost certainly would. Suddenly Avis was aware of an enormous relief. She began to laugh and went on laughing as she finished drying her hair and started to pack, with a heart lighter than it had been for months.

She was free—free—and it was wonderful. How easy it was, she reflected, to drift into a situation that you really didn't want. She might have drifted into an engagement with Robert and never realised until it was too late that it was for all the wrong reasons. Surely there was such a thing as love— romantic love that swept you off your feet—in spite of what the cynics said. There must be—it was too good not to be true.

She sat down again beside the fire to finish drying her hair and thought about love. *Was* there nothing more than sex, as most people seemed to think these days? Sex would be wonderful, she was sure, with the right man, and that was worth waiting for. But there must be something more than sex, something added on that you couldn't define, that made one man different from every other man in the world.

Her brooding on this important subject was interrupted by the arrival of the elder of her two flatmates, Jane Carter. Jane was tall and angular, with an earnest face and no sense of humour. She was engaged to a young man called Kenneth, who was one day going to be an accountant, when he had passed his exams. They were going to be married soon and live in two rooms in Kenneth's parents' house, which Jane called 'our flat' and which she was painstakingly planning, down to the last hook in the wardrobe that Kenneth was making from a do-it-yourself kit.

'Hullo, Jane, you're early. I thought you were going to the flicks?' Avis gave her hair its last brushing and stood up.

Jane hung up her mac on the kitchen door. 'Kenneth wanted to go home to study, so I thought I'd do some sewing.' She took the sewing machine from its case and scrambled under the table to fix the plug in its socket. She was making her own dress for her wedding, spending many weeks on it and much deliberation. It was a fine woollen, in a pale beige, which she could wear for 'best' later on, she said, and which wouldn't show the dirt.

'Had a good day?' she enquired absently, spreading her sewing out on the kitchen table.

'Eventful,' said Avis. 'Mr Hanworthy wants me to fly to the South of France, to take some documents to one of his valued clients, and I'm to stay a week.'

'Oh, really? That'll be nice for you.' Jane peered shortsightedly at the machine-needle, which she was trying unsuccessfully to thread.

'Let me do it for you.' Avis threaded the needle neatly.

'Thanks.' Jane looked up, bringing her attention to what Avis had just told her. 'When are you off? Tomorrow? And what does Robert say about it?'

'He's very uptight,' Avis admitted. 'Apparently he was expecting me to go to the Bank dinner with him and feels let down. A pity he didn't remember to mention it earlier,' she added, feeling it necessary to justify herself. Jane had definite ideas about a woman's role and was inclined to deliver lectures at any moment.

She looked rather shocked now. 'Oh, but don't you think you ought to have consulted him first? Men always like to be consulted,' she added primly.

Avis wasn't going to be lured into an argument. 'It all happened very quickly, and Mr Hanworthy insisted on my going.' She bent over the sewing on the table. 'Oh, you've finished the embroidery on the collar. That looks lovely. You've done it beautifully.'

'Do you really think so?' Jane smiled modestly. 'I'm rather pleased with the effect myself.' She smoothed down the embroidery and forgot all about Robert.

Avis went into the bedroom she shared with Janice, thinking briefly about Jane and her Kenneth. Was Jane in love with him—really in love? One couldn't, somehow, imagine Jane letting her hair down, but perhaps she would be happy and contented, making a home, looking after her husband and helping him in his career, sewing pretty clothes for the children. Perhaps, in the long run, that was what marriage was all about. But surely there was more than that?

A few minutes later Janice came rushing into the

bedroom, her curly gold hair in a damp tangle round her cheeky little face. Janice was a small cuddly blonde who worked in the underwear department of the local store and was the life and soul of any party she went to. 'Avis—my angel! What's all this I hear? Jane says you're off to the Riviera tomorrow. How absolutely smashing! It'll be all sunny and warm like the travel ads—blue sea and blue sky—and you'll meet a wonderful man, and he'll fall for you straight away and take you in his arms and——'

'Hey, steady on!' Avis laughed. 'This is a business trip, not an orgy!'

Janice sighed gustily. 'But wouldn't it be lovely if it was? I'd give my new boots for an orgy just now. Since Jed went off to the U.S. I've had no fun, no man, no bed. I'm going to a party tonight at my cousin's, but I expect it'll be horribly proper. My aunt will be there and all the bedroom doors will be locked. Ah poor me!'

Then she cheered up. 'But a gorgeous man came in today to buy some frilly panties. He *said* they were for his sister.' She giggled. 'But he spent quite a time chatting me up before Miss Roberts started casting her eagle eye on me. I've got a feeling he may be back tomorrow.' She waltzed round the room, carolling, 'I took one look at you, that's all I had to do, and then my heart stood still.' She fell on to her bed and pulled off her boots. 'No songs like the old songs, they were so lovely and smoochy.' She rolled on the bed.

Avis cast an affectionate eye on her. 'Sex kitten!' she smiled. 'Don't you ever think of anything else?'

'What else is there to think about?'

Avis held up a cotton dress with a jazzy pattern and frills round the skirt and considered it before replacing it in the wardrobe. *Not* the sort of

garment a secretary would wear on a business trip.
'How about love?' she said.

'Love?' Janice gave a peal of laughter. 'That's
just a fancy word for the same thing.'

'No more than that?'

'You mean——?' Janice jerked her head towards
the sitting room from whence came the whirr of
the sewing machine. 'Marriage is real, marriage is
earnest, all changing nappies and warming hubby's
slippers? Dead boring!' She lay back on the bed
and put her hands behind her head. 'No, love, you
stick to the Riviera if you're looking for Romance
with a capital R. Think of the topless beaches and
the casinos and the little cafés hidden away among
the palm trees. Lucky, lucky Avis, why don't I
work for a nice solicitor? I don't see Miss Roberts
sending me off on a holiday to the South of
France.'

Avis grinned. 'It sounds terrific the way you put
it, Jan, but I expect it will be all work, and reading
the newspaper to old Mrs Clavell. She probably
asked for me because she wants to get a free
secretary-companion for a week.'

But next day, as she sat in the plane watching
the coastline of England slip away beneath her, she
felt a rising excitement. Perhaps it was just leaving
the cold and wet behind, or perhaps it was this
new, heady feeling of being free and able to please
herself (which she had almost forgotten about
since she started to go out with Robert) but now
she could at least dream about a wonderful man
who would turn her knees to jelly and her world
into a rainbow-coloured heaven on earth. Briefly
she thought of Robert and reflected that at no
time had he had the slightest effect on her knees or
her perception of the world around her.

Ah well, there was no harm in dreaming, she

thought, her mouth quirking with amusement, and
it passed the time. So as the plane bore her
southwards she closed her eyes and indulged in
thrilling fantasies of a tall dark stranger with lean
muscular hips and a gorgeous sun-tan. Perhaps,
after all, she thought, Janice was right, and sex was
all there was to love. She wondered if she could
love a man who was small and tubby with a pink
face and a squeaky voice.

The first thing she noticed as she emerged from
the plane in Nice was the change in temperature.
After an English February it seemed really warm
and all the women in the large, modern airport
were wearing light clothes. In London, when she
left, it had been even wetter than yesterday, with a
cold, sneaky wind that whipped round your
ankles. It had been difficult to know what to wear
for travelling, especially as she had elected to
travel light and pack everything she might need for
the week in one small travelling case, together with
the satchel that she could take inside the plane
with her. In the end she had settled for a
businesslike jersey two-piece in chestnut-brown,
with a patterned silk scarf knotted at the neck.
Getting to Heathrow had been accomplished with
the aid of a fashionable mac with a gathered yoke,
which could double for a topcoat if necessary, and
a mushroom umbrella, but her new court shoes
had got soaked. Once in the plane she had
changed into her only other pair of shoes—
flimsy sandals with thin ankle straps and ridicul-
ously high heels. She had bought them hastily
yesterday when she left the office. Every woman
who could afford to winter on the Riviera would
be wildly glamorous, of course, and though she
couldn't hope to compete with the rich darlings of
society she could try to look passable.

If she could have seen herself as she stepped from the plane she wouldn't have worried. She had what every woman around might envy—a look of untouched youth, a freshness of perfect skin and slender body, and a glowing eagerness in the glinting sherry-brown eyes that looked around her for the driver, who, she had been informed by phone, would meet her from the plane and escort her to Mrs Clavell's villa outside Menton.

'Mees Brown?' A small dark man in loose trousers and a denim jacket appeared at her side. When she nodded he announced, 'I am Jacques. Madame 'ave sent me to drive you to her house.'

Avis smiled thank you and he grinned widely and smoothed back his shiny black hair. 'This is all the luggage, yes?' Jacques looked surprised but pleased. No doubt most of Mrs Clavell's rich guests came equipped with stacks of cases groaning with trendy clothes.

Avis sat beside Jacques in the front of the large saloon car. The little Frenchman was talkative and was obviously proud of his English, which was really very good, as he had not, he was anxious to inform her, visited her country yet. 'But we have the *touristes* all the year—Engleesh and American—and Madame Clavell she is kind and teach me. One day I intend to visit America and make my fortune.' His white teeth gleamed in a face the colour of a walnut shell.

Avis laughed. 'If I were you, Jacques, I should stay where you are. Fortunes aren't made so easily in America as they once were, they tell me, and this is a heavenly place.'

She feasted her eyes on the passing scenery: the little blue bays pinched between one promontory and the next, with fishing boats bobbing at anchor; the small towns they passed through, which Jacques named for her—Villefranche, Cap Ferrat, Beaulieu-sur-Mer.

'It would be possible to travel by the motor road,' he told her, 'but Madame say I drive too fast on the motor road.' He pulled a face like a naughty monkey. 'So she insist I bring you on the lower corniche, which is so pretty, *n'est-ce pas?*'

'It is indeed.' Avis was entranced. She had been abroad twice before. Once with her mother, which was the last holiday they had had together before her mother remarried and went off to live in Australia. And once—last year when she was missing her mother rather badly—she had treated herself to a week's tour of the Greek islands. But this place was different from either. It had a character all its own, this strip of fantastic beauty lying between the sea and the blue-green mountains rising up on the left. And the mimosa! In February! Its perfume was in the air and its branches, laden with their yellow fluffs of blossom, hung over every wall and hedge. Avis sighed with delight.

Jacques was pleased with her enthusiasm. 'It is good that you like our scenery. Madame Clavell, she tell me, "Mees Brown, we must make her happy with us, Jacques." '

'That's very kind of her,' Avis murmured, a little puzzled that such care should be taken to make a fuss of a mere solicitor's secretary, who had come out purely on business.

At last they drove through Menton, Jacques pointing out various details as they went. 'There is the old town which is very near to Italy. A stone-throw, you say, yes?' He laughed at his own expertise with the language. 'Here fishermen live and the streets are narrow. But the new town is very—how you say?—very smart. It 'as hotels—

very expensive—and a casino and place for the yachts. A mar—mar——'

'Marina?'

'That is so—a marina. I see you, too, help me with my Engleesh, Mees Brown.'

Avis smiled, liking the little man's enthusiasm, and promised to do what she could in the short time she would be staying. 'Just a week,' she said.

'A week only?' Jacques sounded surprised. 'But Madame 'as said—ah well, I 'ave not understood.'

They left the sea behind and the car began to climb a steep, twisty road up into the hills, so steep that Avis held her breath when she looked down the way they had come. In places trees overhung the road, turning it into a dark green tunnel, and now and then she caught a glimpse between the lush foliage of villas that looked as if they came from a fairy-tale world where houses are made of icing sugar.

At last the car turned in between high gateposts and Jacques announced triumphantly, 'We are 'ere, safe and sound, Mees Brown.' He jumped out and opened the door for Avis.

Mrs Clavell's villa had an exotic appearance, which was absolutely right in its setting; a low white house built into the slope of the hill, with wings at irregular angles. A wild garden tumbled down over rocks, rioting with huge-leaved sub-tropical plants, and Avis could see a veranda round the side, overlooking the garden, with brightly-striped canvas loungers and a swinging hammock. Mrs Clavell must indeed be (as Mr Hanworthy had wryly declared) loaded, to own such a villa, as well as an estate in England. Lucky Mrs Clavell, Avis thought.

Jacques led the way into a cool, uncluttered hall with black-and-white tiles, which gave it the appearance of a Dutch painting. A young woman in a chic striped cotton dress appeared from the back quarters. 'This is my wife, Marie,' Jacques told Avis. 'Marie will not speak English,' he lamented. 'I try to learn her, but she say *Pouf!* and that is all.' He smiled winningly. 'Per'aps you can learn her, Mees Brown?'

Avis smiled doubtfully. 'Perhaps.' She turned to Marie and tried her O-level French. 'Will you please show me my room, Marie?'

Marie smiled. She looked attractive when she grinned, like a pretty little monkey. *'Mais certainement, mademoiselle.'* She picked up Avis's case and led the way across the lobby and up a shallow flight of stairs.

The bedroom into which Avis was shown was fresh and dainty, with pink and white daisies on the bedspread and curtains, and a breathtaking view. She walked over to the open window and the scents of the garden came up to meet her. 'Oh, how absolutely super!' she breathed in delight.

Marie creased her brow. *'Pardon?'*

'Super,' repeated Avis, pointing to the view from the window, over the green and gold and silver of the trees and bushes, down, down, to a vividly blue strip of sea beyond, under a paler blue sky. *'C'est très-très——'* She waved her hand helplessly, unable to find a word in French. *'Très joli,'* she said, inadequately. And then she laughed. 'Very pretty' was totally inadequate to express her delight.

'Oui,' agreed Marie politely, looking slightly puzzled. No doubt the view had ceased to impress her.

She lifted Avis's bag on to an ottoman at the foot of the bed and unpacked it in silence. If she was surprised at the modest contents, she made no remark upon it, although doubtless she was accustomed to visitors arriving equipped with bags full of stunning clothes. When she had finished she told Avis that Madame took tea at half-past three in the *salon* and would Mademoiselle please come down when she was ready?

At half past three promptly Avis made her way downstairs, taking with her the large sealed envelope containing the papers from Mr Hanworthy. A door stood open, leading into a large, airy room that she took to be the *salon*. A low table was set for tea, so this must be right. A sofa was pulled up to the table, but Mrs Clavell was not there. Avis put the envelope on the table and stood uncertainly behind the sofa while the minutes passed, feeling the awkwardness of being left alone in a strange house. Then suddenly she was aware that she wasn't alone. She had the strangest feeling that someone was behind her. She spun round to see a tall, lean man lounging in the window alcove, hands in pockets, half hidden by the long blue damask curtains. He must have been standing there watching her in silence from the moment she came into the room. She met a level, unsmiling gaze, but he didn't move or speak, just went on watching her out of half-narrowed eyes that, from this distance, looked steely grey.

And then it happened, just as she had pictured it on the plane. She put her hand out to the back of the sofa as her knees went to jelly and her breath caught almost painfully in her throat. It was an entirely new sensation.

'Oh, I—I didn't see you,' she gasped.

He strolled out lazily, eyeing her with an amused gleam in his eyes. Her impression was that he wasn't really handsome; impressive, rather, in a lean, greyhound sort of way. He wore superbly cut dark pants and a paisley silk shirt. *'Really?'* he said smoothly, as if he didn't believe her.

The effect of the shock was subsiding now and Avis found herself resenting something in his tone, an ironic, patronising note.

'Yes, really,' she said very coolly.

He nodded. 'If you say so. You, I take it, are Miss Ava Brown, the girl my mother has produced from Hanworthy's office?'

Produced! What a very odd word to use!

'I am Mr Hanworthy's secretary,' she said. 'And my name is *Avis* Brown.'

'Ah—Avis. My mother got it wrong, then. She quite often gets things muddled, does my dear mama, you must be prepared for that.' There was a pause. 'Avis!' He looked up at the ceiling and then down at her. 'Meaning a bird, of course. "The early bird that catches the worm," is that it?' He held out a hand. 'Allow me to introduce myself. Holt Clavell, at your service, *mademoiselle*.' He inclined his head, still with that ironic gleam in his eye.

'How do you do, Mr Clavell.' Avis put her hand in his. His fingers were cool and strong, and she pulled her hand away quickly, feeling as if she had touched a live electric wire. So this was Holt Clavell, the brilliant young barrister that Mr Hanworthy had enthused about. Avis could see what he meant. She wouldn't fancy standing in the witness box, being cross-examined by this man with the long, clever face and magnetic eyes, which she saw on closer inspection had a smoky tinge to the grey and a lighter rim to the irises, giving them a curiously magnetic look. And did he always talk in riddles? 'I'm not sure what you mean to imply by catching worms,' she said calmly. 'But "Avis" does not, I believe, mean a bird. It's a medieval name, originally the Norman Havoise.' One up to me, I think, Mr Holt Clavell.

A gleam that might have been amusement came into the strange grey eyes. 'Wow!' he said, somehow the slang word came strangely from him. 'And I'm sure you can tell me the original meaning, Miss Brown, as you seem to be so well informed.'

'Certainly. The original meaning was "refuge in war",' said Avis, her wide sherry-brown eyes meeting his innocently. 'That always reassures me.'

'Do you indulge in many wars, Miss Brown?'

'I have yet to fight a war.' She smiled sweetly at him. *But I get a feeling I could fight with you. And then I'd certainly need that refuge.*

He gave her a smile that didn't reach his eyes. 'We're having such a fascinating conversation that I forget my manners. Won't you sit down, Miss Brown?' He indicated a deep, chintz-covered chair beside the tea table, and Avis sat down rather stiffly.

He stood in front of the carved marble mantelpiece. 'Has anyone told my mother that you're here?'

'I don't know. Marie said that Mrs Clavell has tea at three-thirty.'

He nodded. 'Mama is very particular about her tea.' He smiled. 'Like all good Britons abroad. She has it sent specially from Fortnums in London when she's in residence here. I trust you, too, enjoy tea, Miss Brown, and haven't succumbed to the habit of drinking coffee on all occasions?'

'I'm simply dying for a cup of tea,' Avis confessed candidly.

'Splendid! I'll go in search of Mama, then.' He turned to the door and then came back. 'You know, of course, that my mother is something of an invalid?'

'Mr Hanworthy did mention——' Avis began rather vaguely. Mr Hanworthy had implied that Mrs Clavell was also something of a hypochondriac, but she couldn't very well refer to that.

Her son's eyes narrowed in affectionate amusement. 'Mama is noted for producing ailments very conveniently. But don't let that embarrass you, Miss Brown. She's quite blatant about it. In other words, she knows that we know.'

'Oh, really?' Avis murmured. 'It sounds rather complicated.' But she didn't think he heard. He had already gone from the room, leaving the door open.

Almost immediately she heard footsteps approaching across the tiled hall. Then a woman's voice murmuring something and Holt Clavell answering, quite loudly and clearly, 'Well, at least, Mama, she's an improvement on the last one.'

There was a ssh-ing sound from the woman and Avis got to her feet as mother and son appeared in the doorway together. Mrs Clavell wore a dress of flowered silky material which hung loosely round a figure that appeared to Avis to be thinner than she remembered, from seeing her briefly in London. She came across the room to Avis, walking slowly and holding out her hand.

'My dear Miss Brown—how good of you to come all this way! I do apologise for not being here. Marie didn't tell me you'd arrived. I hope my son has made you welcome.' She smiled warmly, and Avis thought once again how lovely she was. With her delicate colouring and exquisite bonestructure she looked like an actress who had once been a raving beauty but whose looks had begun

to fade, while the sweetness of her expression had
remained. Her eyes were like her son's, smoky grey
with long black lashes, and they had a humorous
twinkle that was definitely missing in his.

As Avis's hand was enclosed in a friendly grasp
she noticed that Mrs Clavell's fingers were chilly
for such a warm day. 'Oh yes, thank you,' she said
politely, not looking at the tall, urbane man
standing in silence beside his mother. She wished
she were not so conscious of him; his very presence
made her nerves tingle.

Marie came in with a tea-tray then and set it on
the low table. Tea in a silver pot; buttered scones
with jam and cream; a mouthwatering chocolate
layer cake. Avis was afraid her tummy would start
to rumble; it seemed a long time since breakfast and she had eaten practically nothing on the
plane.

'Tea is my favourite meal,' her hostess said,
sinking on to the sofa. 'Holt dear, would you get
my shawl from my room. I left it up there when I'd
had my rest.'

Holt went out and returned with a cobweb-fine
knitted shawl, lifted his mother's legs carefully to
the sofa and draped the shawl over them. 'There,'
he said, with a little pat. 'Comfy?'

'Thank you, dear, beautifully.' Mrs Clavell gave
him an upward look of undisguised fondness.
'Now, do sit down, Miss Brown. Or wouldn't it be
more friendly to call you Ava?'

'Her name is Avis, Mama,' her son put in in a
laconic voice.

'Ah! You two young people have got to know
each other already! Now, isn't that charming?'

'Is it, Mama?' He regarded his mother mock-
ingly, dark brows lifted. She hunched one shoulder
and turned it upon him and then directed her

glance to Avis. 'My son is a terrible tease, Avis. You mustn't take him seriously. Now, my dear, will you be very kind and pour out the tea? My hands aren't as strong as they used to be.'

Holt Clavell put a hand on his mother's shoulder. 'I must ask you to excuse me, Mama. I have work to get through.'

'Oh, but Holt dear, aren't you going to join us for tea?' Mrs Clavell's mouth drooped.

'I think not,' he said with a faint smile. 'I'm sure you two ladies will have much to discuss, without my presence. Isn't that so, Miss Brown?'

Deliberately he turned his gaze on Avis, a calculating gaze with a hint of malice in it. For a long moment she managed to hold his look, and the strangest stirring began inside her, as if her body was being taken over by a force that she couldn't withstand. She saw him in photographic detail—the long, clever face; the dark hair, flicked back behind his ears and just touching the collar of his paisley silk shirt; the watchful, thick-lashed eyes. The mouth——

As her glance rested on his mouth, with its firm, frankly sensual lower lip, the stirring inside became a tumult and she lowered her eyes, putting down her cup with a little clatter.

'Why, yes, I suppose so,' she muttered through dry lips, feeling as if the words were being dragged out of her. This must be the way he operated in court, and at this moment she felt as if she were in the witness stand.

Worse—she felt as if she were the prisoner in the dock and that he was cleverly extracting a 'guilty' plea from her.

Guilty of what? She wished she knew. Her heart began to thump most uncomfortably, and only returned to normal gradually when he had gone from the room and the door was closed behind him.

And yet, without his strong masculine presence, the room seemed curiously empty, the vista of sky and sea outside the window a less vivid blue.

CHAPTER TWO

MRS CLAVELL's eyes followed her son to the door and she sighed. Then she turned her attention back to Avis, with a rueful smile. 'Holt only arrived yesterday, but already he has to work. He tells me he is very busy preparing a new brief and I understand that, of course, but it's so lovely to see him. I suppose I'm just a possessive mother.' The twinkle came into her eyes and Avis found herself taking to the older woman. There was something immediately likeable about her—an unaffected naturalness that was rather rare in the rich women clients she had encountered in the course of her job, who were usually very demanding and haughty.

She poured her hostess's tea—very weak with no milk or sugar—and passed her the plate of scones. Mrs Clavell sighed again. 'I shouldn't really. My weight is beginning to soar again, since I haven't been taking much exercise lately.'

'But you have a lovely figure,' Avis broke in impulsively, and then remembered that Mr Hanworthy had said that Mrs Clavell was a bit of a hypochondriac, and if that were true then she probably *would* be unnecessarily diet-conscious.

Her hostess's smile was a little twisted. 'Thank you, my dear, but unfortunately my doctor is a trifle worried about me, which is a frightful bore, but I have to take her seriously and try to do as I'm told.'

She took a scone and urged Avis to make a hearty tea. 'Don't stand on ceremony, my dear, I'm sure you have a healthy young appetite. Now, sit back and be comfy and tell me all about yourself. You live at home with your parents?'

Avis shook her head. 'I share a flat with two other girls. My father died when I was a baby and my mother married again just over a year ago. She's living in Australia.' She sighed.

'And you miss her very much?'

'I do indeed. We were great friends when I grew up, and we used to do things together.' The brown eyes were cloudy. 'I could have gone with them to Australia, she wanted me to, but——' she shrugged '—I didn't think it was quite on.' Suddenly she found she could talk to this woman. There was something about her that reminded her of her mother. 'I thought she and my new stepfather needed time to be together and get settled down.'

Mrs Clavell nodded. 'Very wise of you. And very mature, if I may say so, for a girl of——?'

'I'm twenty. Twenty-one just after Christmas.' She was silent for a moment, remembering, and then she said impulsively, 'Christmas is the worst time to be on your own. Both my flatmates were away last Christmas and I hung up some holly, cooked a nice little dinner and looked at the telly.' She pulled a face. 'Goodness, that sounds feeble and self-pitying, but I wasn't really sorry for myself. I told myself that there would be lots of lovely Christmases ahead.'

'And so there will be,' said Mrs Clavell, 'if you believe it. I can see you're a romantic, Avis, and that makes two of us.' She laughed. She had a fascinating laugh, low and musical. In fact, Avis found herself thinking, her hostess had a warm, delightful personality. She wondered how she could have such a chilling son. 'Is Mr—er—is Holt your only child?' she enquired.

Mrs Clavell shook her head. 'Oh no, I have one other son—Peter. Peter is twenty-nine—three years younger than Holt and already married with two children. Two little boys.' She smiled wryly. 'I'm afraid I'm that unnatural woman, one who doesn't dote on her grandchildren. Real little horrors, they are!'

There didn't seem to be any answer to that, and as Mrs Clavell seemed for the moment to be lost in thought, Avis munched her second scone and said nothing. After a minute or two her hostess blinked and said, 'Oh dear, I'm being very remiss. Won't you have a slice of cake? Marie makes the most delicious chocolate cake and she gets so disappointed if it isn't eaten. I really can't allow myself all those calories, and Holt hasn't much of a sweet tooth.'

No, Avis thought, I can't see that lean, elegant body being nourished on chocolate cake. He would be a steak-and-salad man, with some exotic cheese to follow, and he would allow himself a moderate amount of vintage wine.

She jerked her attention back to her hostess. What was she thinking of—brooding over that arrogant Holt Clavell's taste in food?

Tea-time passed pleasantly. Avis had three cups of tea and two slices of Marie's chocolate cake, which was indeed delicious. Mrs Clavell seemed eager to talk. She told Avis about her husband, who had been more than twenty years older than she, and had died two years ago. About his father, who had started a business of his own in the jewellery trade in Birmingham, and his grandfather who had bought the family house in the Cotswolds, over a hundred years ago.

'And you still go back to England?' Avis asked. For some reason she had begun to feel quite involved with the Clavell family.

'Oh, yes indeed, every summer. It gets much too hot here for me and Menton is so full of visitors. England is my real home. My husband and I were so happy together there and the boys were born there. It was his greatest wish——' She broke off, her voice suddenly choked. She took a sip of tea and then smiled at Avis ruefully. 'I get sentimental, thinking of home. To me it's the most beautiful place. Look, I'll show you——'

She took a red leather album from the low table near her and passed it to Avis. 'All the photographs there are of Dell Cottage.'

Avis turned the pages of the album, her interest quickening. Dell Cottage had been lovingly documented over the years. The earliest photographs were in black and white, fading now to sepia, the later ones in colour, and they obviously traced the life of the cottage and its occupants from way back in the last century.

Cottage! It might have started small, but it had obviously been extended over the years and it looked to Avis now more like a mansion. She turned the pages to the latest photograph and saw a beautiful, graceful building of mellow Cotswold stone, long and low, with high, twisty chimneys, nestling against a background of tall old trees. Lawns spread out green and smooth as billiard tables. Roses and flowering shrubs overflowed from the surrounding beds. What looked like a family party was taking tea under a spreading tree on the right of the lawn and in the lower left-hand corner could be seen the edge of a pool, with rocks and waterlilies and tall irises.

'My husband was a keen gardener,' Mrs Clavell said. 'He was very proud of his garden.' She leaned towards Avis, pointing. 'That is he—the one with the linen hat. And that's Holt, standing

behind him. It was taken on a day of celebration—
Holt had just heard that he'd passed his final
exams for the Bar. That's Peter, my younger son,
and his wife Hazel. They'd been married only a
month or two.'

Something in the way she said 'Hazel' made
Avis glance quickly at her. Mrs Clavell had no
great love for her daughter-in-law, that was quite
plain. Avis looked from the fair young man,
sprawling languidly in a hammock chair, to the
woman standing behind him, one hand possessively
on his shoulder, her pale hair brushed severely
away from her face, her eyes looking straight at
the camera without a hint of a smile.

'It's a beautiful house,' she said, tactfully
avoiding any reference to personalities. 'I don't
wonder you love it.' She went on studying the
photograph, but now it wasn't the house she was
fixing her gaze on. It was a tall, lanky man in
shorts and white shirt, leaning nonchalantly
against the trunk of the tree, a tea-cup in his hand,
looking relaxed, faintly arrogant. There was no
sign of relief or excitement about his attitude that
might have been expected of a young man who
had just taken the first long, difficult step along
the road of a demanding career. But Holt Clavell
wouldn't expect to fail, he wasn't a loser.

Mrs Clavell seemed to be back in the past again
and Avis said tentatively, 'I've brought the papers
that Mr Hanworthy thought you might need, Mrs
Clavell. They're all in this packet.' She placed it on
the table beside the tea-tray.

Her hostess blinked as if in surprise. 'The
papers? Oh yes, of course. I can't be bothered with
them now—can't concentrate in the afternoon. I'm
at my best and brightest in the morning. Perhaps
tomorrow morning—or the day after,' she added

rather vaguely, leaving Avis puzzled. Mrs Clavell's request to Mr Hanworthy had been so urgent—and now she seemed scarcely interested.

But a moment later she sat up eagerly as the door opened and her son Holt came into the room. Avis felt her heart give a jolt, and she caught her breath. He really was rather breath-taking, with his height and his lazy good looks, and his air of complete composure and self-assurance. She wondered how he looked in court, in wig and gown. Sensational, she was sure of it.

He helped himself to a scone. 'Had a nice chat?' he enquired of his mother, and there was the faintly mocking tone to his words again.

If Mrs Clavell noticed it she ignored it. 'Lovely,' she said happily. 'Avis and I have been getting to know each other and she's been looking at all the old photographs of Dell Cottage.'

'Ah!' Her son's mouth pulled into a judicial line and he nodded his dark head up and down. 'And I'm sure Avis approved; Didn't you, Avis?'

There was no doubt about the mockery now and as the magnetic grey eyes fixed themselves on her thoughtfully Avis found herself wanting to yell at him, 'What's the matter with me? Why do you look at me like that, as if I was a criminal?' But instead she said tightly, 'I think it's a lovely house.'

He laughed aloud, and she couldn't think why he found her remark so amusing. 'I bet you do,' he said dryly, and turned to his mother.

'I'm driving down to Menton, Mama. I need some more writing paper. Is there anything I can get for you?'

Mrs Clavell beamed happily. 'How lucky, Holt. I've run out of silks for my work. I need the pink—the salmon pink, not the rose pink, you'll

need to match it. And some more of the dark
purple——' She was rummaging in a workbasket
as she spoke. 'I'll try and find a pattern. And if
you could ask them whether the black wool has
come in yet—they were expecting it today,
and——'

'Hey, steady on, Mama, you can't entrust me
with an errand like that! Can't Marie get it for you
when she goes home this evening?'

Mrs Clavell bit her lip in annoyance. 'I specially
wanted to finish the table-mats today. I've only
got one more to do.' She tapped her fingers on the
arm of the sofa, looking round as if she could find
the silks she wanted somewhere hidden in the
room. Then her glance fell on Avis and she smiled
suddenly. 'Ah—Avis, my dear, you could cope
with this little errand, I'm sure. Embroidery is
women's work, isn't it, Holt? Not for the mighty
male to concern himself with.' Her smile turned to
her son, gently teasing. 'Run Avis down to
Menton with you, there's a good boy. There'll be
plenty of time before dinner. You could show her
round a bit. There, that's settled. Now, Avis, I'll
just give you the patterns——'

Five minutes later Avis found herself sitting
beside Holt in the big saloon car that Jacques had
driven from the airport. A glance at the chiselled
profile of the man at the wheel told her nothing,
but she was quite sure he was *not* pleased to have
her as a passenger. He drove as fast as he dared
down the steep twisty hill, and didn't say a word
until he had found a parking meter. He switched
off the engine and turned to Avis. 'Menton,' he
said, in a studiedly ironic tone and with a little
wave of his hand. 'Or do you require a guided
tour, Miss Brown?'

'I don't require anything—from you, Mr

Clavell,' Avis said stiffly, 'except to be pointed in the direction of the shops where I can buy the silks for your mother.' Her heart was hammering uncomfortably; this man and his calculated rudeness was having a cataclysmic effect on her.

He didn't move, just sat back studying her face in a way that made the blood scald her cheeks. 'It was a clever ploy of my mama's, don't you think? Evidently she's exhausted all the girls in our own set and now she's fishing in the typing pool. A neat little trap, but I have no intention of falling into it.'

She glared at him, her skin prickling with anger. 'I haven't the least idea what you're talking about, Mr Clavell. Now, if you'll please——'

'Don't give me that, my girl, you know damn well what I'm talking about, and I may as well make it quite clear from the beginning that there's nothing doing. My mama means well and I adore her extremely, but she has the wrong idea altogether, and if she's given you the impression that I'm to be caught like a fish on the hook of the latest little bit of nothing with a pretty face and good legs, you can forget it.' His eyes travelled down and rested on Avis's slender legs stretched out beneath the dashboard.

For a moment or two she was speechless with rage. Then the adrenalin began to flow. Reaching out to the door-handle, she said in a low, furious voice, 'Will you please point out the shop to me, Mr Clavell, and then I'll leave you. I expect I can get a taxi back to your mother's house. I find you odious and disgustingly offensive, and I really don't wish to be in your company a minute longer than necessary.' She fumbled with the handle, to no avail; the car door remained securely closed.

Holt Clavell surveyed her with a small ironic

smile. 'Well, well, well, the kitten has claws! It's no good manhandling that door catch, it locks on the inside.'

She felt as if she would suffocate if she had to stay a moment longer in the front seat of the car in such close proximity to this hateful individual. 'Let me out, then!' she hissed.

'All in good time.' He leaned back in his corner and the cold grey eyes fixed themselves judicially upon her face. Avis turned deliberately, and looked out of the window. Outside, luxury cars glided along the wide avenue, under a row of feathery palms. People in colourful light clothing strolled along as if they had all the time in the world to spare (which they probably had.) On one side of the avenue tall white houses and hotels climbed up the hill, tier after tier. On the other, the blue water glittered silvery in the sunlight. All was easy and peaceful. But inside the car the tension built up moment by moment like a time-bomb, until Avis thought she would scream.

'Look at me.' Holt's hand came out and gripped her chin, turning her face towards him, with a strength that she couldn't resist. 'Are you seriously suggesting that you knew nothing of my mama's plot when you came here?'

The touch of his fingers on her face was doing very strange things to her breathing and her voice was two tones higher than usual as she snapped, 'You're not in court now, Mr Barrister Clavell, and I don't see why I should be cross-questioned, but for the record I'm not *seriously suggesting* anything.' Her lip curled. 'I'm stating quite definitely that I know nothing of any plot to catch you, as you so elegantly put it. I haven't the slightest wish to "catch" a man, and even if I had, you, Mr Clavell, would be at the bottom of my list. Not even *on* my list, in fact,' she added, with satisfaction. Her cheeks were hot, and her heart was thumping, but she felt she had held her own against this intolerable man.

'Well,' she said, 'are you going to let me out?'

Again the ironic smile. 'Quite an articulate young woman, aren't you, Avis Brown?' he said.

'I don't take that as a compliment, and I don't like being patronised,' said Avis loftily. 'And I think we've come to the end of this conversation, so will you *please* let me out and show me the shop.'

'All in good time,' he said again soothingly. 'I don't agree that we've come to the end of the conversation. I think we have several things to discuss.'

Avis lifted her chin. 'I have nothing to discuss with you, Mr Clavell.'

'Put it another way, then,' he said with exaggerated patience. 'I think we have several things to get straight.'

She sat in silence, her back rigid, disdaining even to lean against the soft leather of the car seat.

'You see,' he went on, and the grey eyes ran over her consideringly, 'I've been plagued by Mama's alluring protégées for more than a year now. It seemed to me not only probable but certain that you were yet another of them. If it turns out that I've been wrong I'll owe you an apology. Certainly, now I come to think of it, she didn't give me the usual build-up when she said you were coming. I expect she wanted to push me off balance when I saw you.' He went on examining her face as if she were a specimen under a microscope.

'Push *you* off balance?' Avis said, giving him a cold look. 'I can't imagine that happening.'

'Oh, it might,' he said lightly. 'I'm a very normal man, and you're an unusually lovely girl. I'm quite sure that Mama has been up to her tricks again, whether she let you in on it or not. In the circumstances I thought it only fair to warn you that I'm not in the market for marriage.'

'That,' said Avis contemptuously, 'couldn't concern me less.'

'You have a—er—a boy-friend already? But of course you have, several probably.'

She shrugged, saying nothing. Let him make what he liked of that. Her thoughts went momentarily to Robert and she could hardly remember what he looked like. Her lips pulled into a little smile because all she could remember clearly was the way his umbrella dripped water down her neck.

'Ah,' said Holt Clavell, 'I see I'm right. Well, that makes things easier, doesn't it?' There was a little silence, then he said, 'Would you be prepared to tell me how it happened—what led up to your coming here?'

Avis lifted her prettily-marked eyebrows. 'I'm not on oath at the moment, you know, but if you ask me very politely I'll tell you.'

'Please, Miss Brown,' he said solemnly, 'will you give me the information?'

She'd been wrong about the laughter-lines. They were there round his eyes, very faintly, when he smiled.

'Well——' she began, making her words precise, as if she were giving evidence, 'as I recall, your mother wrote to say she needed to have all her papers brought down here and that she wanted me, specially, to bring them. It seemed rather odd that she should ask for me particularly, but I did help her in various small ways last time she was in England, when she visited the office. I made her tea, and got her a taxi, and so on. I supposed she felt I wasn't a stranger. And of course when Mr Hanworthy gave me the opportunity to come to the Riviera for a few days I accepted with pleasure.' She sat back in her seat. 'That's all. Satisfied—or does the cross-examination continue?'

'I'm satisfied.'

'And do you believe I'm telling the truth?'

The thin, clever face was enigmatic. 'Ah, that's a question you should never ask a barrister,' he said.

She nodded. 'Forget it,' she said. 'It really isn't of any importance to me.'

'Good,' he said briskly. 'Let's call a truce, then, shall we, and get on with the shopping.' He leaned across to work the safety-catch of the door and his arm brushed against her breast under the thin jacket of her suit. She caught her breath as her inside moved convulsively. She had a brief, vivid memory of Janice lying on her bed in the flat carolling, 'I took one look at you, that's all I had to do, and then my heart stood still.' But of course she hadn't fallen in love at first sight with Holt Clavell; the idea was quite absurd. It was merely that his arrogant masculinity touched some physical chord in her, that was all.

He came round and opened the door for her and she stepped out, pretending not to notice his hand outstretched to help her, not daring to let him touch her again.

'Thank you.' She glanced briefly up at the strong, clever face, at the firm chin, at the mouth that looked so different now that he wasn't pulling it into an ironic smile—different and exciting. Stop it, Avis, she told herself. The magnetism is one-way only. The pin moves towards the magnet. It doesn't work the other way round.

Holt locked the car. 'Come along then, I'll show you the wonders of Menton shopping.' He linked his arm loosely in hers in a way that was friendly, nothing more, and Avis walked beside him in a daze, feeling as if her knees were made of plastic foam.

She took in very little of the glittering Menton shopping centre. Somehow—she never knew how—she matched Mrs Clavell's silks, relying on Holt to do the talking (in French) and pay the bill. Then she went with him to the shop where he bought a large packet of paper. After that she found herself back in the car beside him. He glanced at his watch. 'Just in time for a drink before we go back. I'll take you to my favourite dive, up in the hills.'

Avis hesitated. 'Hadn't we better go back to your mother? She might be waiting for those embroidery silks.'

'Oh, I don't think so. She's not really so hooked on embroidery as all that. Sending you for the silks was just one of her ploys to get us together. Even if you weren't in on the game, Avis Brown, the game is still very much on so far as my dear mama is concerned.' He looked down at her and smiled suddenly. It was the first time he had smiled at her without irony and it made her catch her breath. 'You'll have to be prepared for that.'

Back in the car, Avis felt as if she were living in a dream. She realised vaguely that they were climbing back up the winding road, higher, ever higher, until finally they pulled into a parking space beneath overhanging trees. Holt led the way up a flight of stone steps to a cluster of small buildings, smothered in mimosa and almost hidden in a grove of trees.

'Lemon trees,' he remarked. 'Lemons grow

freely in Menton—it's the warmest spot along the coast.'

'That why they have the Fête du Citron? Jacques was telling me about that when he drove me from the airport, and we saw some of the stands going up.'

Holt grimaced. 'I usually steer clear of all that if I happen to be here in February. The whole town is packed to bursting point at festival time. The actual "do" takes place at the end of the week, so we'll have to take care to keep well out of the way.'

'Oh *no*!' Avis was dismayed. '*I* certainly shan't keep away if I'm still here. I'd love to see it, it sound tremendous fun. I love processions and what Jacques called decoratements.' Her sherry-brown eyes glinted in the sunlight filtering through the trees.

Holt paused on the steps and looked back at her. Then he smiled. 'How old are you, Miss Brown?'

She sighed. 'More questions? I'm twenty—how old are you?'

He looked taken aback for a moment, then he burst out laughing. 'I can give you twelve years,' he said. 'But it feels like thirty at the moment.' He led the way into the small, empty restaurant, leaving her to work that one out.

Avis was enchanted with the place. The room was simply-furnished but spotless. Small tables were already set for dinner, with crisply-laundered white cloths and shining glass and cutlery. There was a horseshoe-shaped bar in the one corner, and the walls were hung with pictures. Avis thought she recognised a Picasso drawing of a nude, done in blue chalk. She stood by the wide window looking down over the green-clad hills, with red roofs nestling here and there deep in the thick foliage, and the wide blue sweep of the sea far below. She said lightly, 'I feel like Cinderella—being wafted from a wet, cold February in London, to a heavenly place like this.'

Holt pulled out a chair for her at a small table. 'Do I qualify as the prince?'

Oh yes, she thought. You would look superb in pale blue satin tunic and knee-breeches and buckled shoes. You have the right air of arrogant distinction. But she was saved from replying by the proprietor appearing from behind the bar, a small, dark man in a white coat. He beamed as he greeted Holt, showing several gold teeth.

'This is my old friend Gaston,' Holt told Avis, 'and he keeps the best cellar in France, as well as being an expert in modern art.'

'*Bonjour. Comment allez-vous?*' Avis tried shyly in her schoolgirl French, holding out her hand.

'*Enchanté, mademoiselle.*' Rather to her embarrassment the little man kissed her hand formally, his dark eyes resting on her in frank admiration.

Holt ordered drinks and then came back and sat opposite her at the small table beside the window, and Gaston brought two glasses on a tray and set it down with a flourish.

'See how you like this,' said Holt, when the little man had departed again. 'It's known as *kir*. If you don't like it I'll get you something else.'

Avis took a sip and looked at him doubtfully. 'Um. What does it taste of?'

'It's blackcurrant *cassis* with white wine. Like it?'

She took another sip and another, and grinned. 'It's rather good. It sort of grows on you.'

'As I do?' He smiled across the table into her

eyes and she felt dazzled. 'You hated me at first, didn't you?'

'Hate's a strong word,' said Avis, looking away. 'I didn't understand why you were being so beastly to me.'

'Self-preservation. I've had to take evading action so often when my mama gets up to her matchmaking ploys that it's almost become automatic. I've no plan to marry, you see. Quite the reverse, in fact.'

'Never?' She managed just the right touch of light amusement.

The faintest of twinkles appeared in the grey eyes. 'Never is a long time, but certainly not until I'm firmly established in my career. That comes first, and it's a very demanding career. You're a solicitor's secretary, I expect you understand that. To have a wife fussing and making demands as well would be the height of folly.'

'Not all wives fuss and make unreasonable demands,' Avis said warmly, feeling it necessary to defend her own sex.

The twinkle disappeared and the cynical look took its place. 'I would question that,' he said lightly. 'But don't let's argue about it. It's a lovely evening—drink up your *kir* and we'll go for a stroll under the lemon trees before we go back for dinner.'

Outside the restaurant narrow rough paths climbed upwards between the trees. Holt led the way and Avis panted after him. Soon the path got steeper and narrower and more overhung with branches and bushes. He stopped. 'I think we're going the wrong way,' he said. 'I thought this path led up to a clearing from where there's a superb view, but I'm afraid I've brought you up in vain. Oh, dear, and your hair's got caught in a branch. Hold quiet and I'll untangle you.'

She stood very still, quivering inside at the touch of his fingers in her hair. It seemed to take a long time, but at last he said, 'There—that's got it. O.K.?'

'Thanks.' She smiled up at him hazily and he was not moving, just standing looking down at her. Their eyes locked and she couldn't look away or move. The silence stretched and stretched and she was scarcely breathing. Then he put both hands on her shoulders and said softly, 'Yes, Miss Avis Brown, you *are* very lovely, and I don't see why Gaston should have all the fun.' He took both her hands and kissed first one and then the other.

Suddenly it seemed unnaturally quiet, just the two of them standing there, enclosed by the dense green leaves. There was only the faint hum of unseen insects in the air. The scent of the mimosa was everywhere. Holt's hands slid up to her shoulders. There was a moment when she could have drawn away, but she was unable to move and he pulled her closer against him. Lethargy invaded her limbs as his hands dropped lower, to her hips, and she found herself pressed back against the rough trunk of a tree.

'Seems a pity to miss such a golden opportunity,' he murmured, and his mouth came down on hers.

She was helpless to resist, even if she had wanted to. But she couldn't respond, either. She just stood there in his arms, her eyes closed, living the moments in a dream while his mouth moved slowly against hers, just as if he were sampling an unfamiliar wine. The kiss seemed to go on for ages and ages, and then it was over. Holt drew away and she sagged against the tree, feeling that he had drawn all the strength from her body with that kiss. She met his eyes mutely, and he was smiling.

'That,' he said, 'is enough for the time being. My natural caution warns me to lay off.'

Just for a moment, Avis was overcome by humiliation. She had only met the man an hour or so ago and yet she had fallen into his arms like a— like a ripe plum! There was only one thing to do and that was to accept what had happened as casually as he obviously did. A girl didn't react with outrage and horror, like some Victorian heroine, if she was kissed. When a man made a pass at you it was supposed to be a compliment, and you just said 'Yes, please,' or 'No, thank you,' as if you were being offered a plate of cakes. Those were the rules of the game and they had served Avis satisfactorily up to now. At least she had never been tempted to say 'Yes, please.' But what did you do when the man's touch melted your flesh and turned your bones to water? The rules didn't help then.

The words of the old song came back into her mind again:

'I took one look at you, that's all I had to do.

And then my heart stood still——'

She heard herself laugh lightly and say, *'My natural caution agrees completely.'*

Holt led the way down the path again, and when they had nearly reached the restaurant he turned, stopping abruptly in his tracks, so that Avis, half sliding down the path behind him, fell into his arms. For a moment he held her closely, laughing down into her face. 'Fate seems determined to throw us together.' He dropped a kiss lightly on her hair and then let her go, straightening her up.

He had been about to say something else when he stopped so suddenly, she was sure of it. But it seemed that she wasn't to know what it was. He didn't speak again until they had climbed back into the car. As he drove down the winding hill he said casually, 'How long are you here for, Avis?'

'I don't quite know. Mr Hanworthy mentioned a week or so. I must speak to you mother about it so that I can book my flight back.'

It was getting dark now, but she could see the way he smiled—it was a satisfied kind of smile. 'By a strange coincidence, I'm here for a week too,' he said. 'I've got a brief to work on, but I can't work twenty-four hours a day. Let's have a good time together, shall we, lovely Avis, and make Mama happy? We both know the score now and it might be rather amusing to play a trick on her. It really would serve her right.'

It took a minute or two for the full import of what he had just said to sink in, but when it did she burst out indignantly, 'If you mean what I think you mean, the answer is No. I'm not quite sure what you mean by "having a good time", but I certainly wouldn't agree to giving your mother the impression that we'd—we'd fallen for each other at first sight. I like your mother, and you don't deceive people you like.'

They had arrived back at the house now and Holt stopped the car and turned off the engine. He said, with a grin, 'Couldn't it be true? Don't you believe in love at first sight?'

'I don't either believe in it or not believe in it,' said Avis crossly. 'I've never experienced it.'

'You're not a romantic, then?'

'I've never thought about that, either,' she said. 'Now, will you please unlatch this complicated door and let me out.'

As he leaned across to unlock the door she drew back in her seat to avoid contact with him, and when the door swung open she almost fell out of the car. It was too dark to see his face, but she thought he was laughing silently.

Mrs Clavell was still reclining on the sofa in the big living room. The long curtains were drawn and the room looked comfortable and welcoming in the soft, concealed lighting. The hi-fi in the corner was playing a Mozart piano sonata. It was near its end and Avis smiled at Mrs Clavell and sat down quietly, enjoying the music, waiting until the last chord died away and the instrument switched itself off.

Mrs Clavell sighed. 'My favourite piece—it always brings me consolation.' For a moment the grey eyes looked oddly desolate and then she smiled at Avis. 'You like Mozart?'

'I love his music,' said Avis. 'It's my favourite too.'

Mrs Clavell looked delighted. 'Then we all share the same taste, Holt as well. We must have a record session while you two are here. After dinner tonight, in fact.'

'That would be very pleasant,' said Avis, rather stiffly. *You two!* Was Mrs Clavell already linking them together in her mind? Was her son right in suspecting that she had brought Avis here with that very end in view? She had been sceptical up to now of his suspicions, thinking that surely if Mrs Clavell were serious in her matchmaking she would choose a girl of her own social standing— not a nobody of a city typist. But now—she wasn't so sure.

She took the embroidery silks from her bag and put them on the table beside her hostess. 'I hope they're the ones you want. And they say the black wool hasn't come in yet but they're expecting it any day, probably tomorrow. I do hope I've got the right colours.'

'Thank you, my dear, these seem exactly right.' Mrs Clavell gave the skeins no more than a casual glance. If she had been anxious to have them she wasn't showing any urgency now. 'It was good of you to go. Marie's talents lie in cooking, and I rather suspect she's almost colour-blind. And Holt is always very masculine and superior if I ask him to do an errand like that for me.' She laughed tolerantly.

There was a little silence and then she reached out and put her hand on Avis's. 'You know, I've always longed for a daughter,' she said. 'A girl to love and buy pretty clothes for. My husband wanted a daughter too.' She sighed. 'But it wasn't to be.'

Avis was at a loss for something to say. 'But you have a daughter-in-law,' she ventured rather shyly.

Mrs Clavell looked very wry. 'Yes,' she said, and her tone was enigmatic enough to remind Avis of her son's pronouncements. 'Yes, I have a daughter-in-law.'

Holt came into the room then and Avis's heart seemed to shift inside her. She hoped this physical response to him wasn't going to last long; it was embarrassing to feel the heat rising into her cheeks and she had a suspicion that Mrs Clavell's gaze was fixed upon her. To assess her reaction to Holt? Oh dear, she was beginning to suspect a motive behind everything her hostess said or did. If he hadn't told her anything of his beastly suspicions she wouldn't have noticed anything out of the ordinary, but as it was the whole situation was quite maddening.

Mrs Clavell put out a hand to her son along the back of the sofa, and he patted it affectionately. 'Have we done our errand to your satisfaction, Mama?'

'Exactly right,' she said, and gave him a little

grin as she added, 'I don't suppose *you* had any hand in the transaction, though.'

'I paid the bill,' he reminded her, lowering himself into a chair and stretching out his long legs, 'but I must admit that Avis was the expert. I get the feeling,' he added, turning his gaze upon Avis, 'that this young lady visitor of ours has many hidden talents—which will no doubt emerge during her stay here.'

His mother chuckled with delight. 'My own impression, too. I'm delighted to hear that her taste in music fits with ours, Holt, and I suggest we have a Mozart session after dinner tonight. What do you say? I have a new record of the Clarinet Quintet which I don't think you've heard. It would be so lovely if we could all share the same pleasure.'

'That would be quite delightful, don't you agree, Avis?' His eyes were still fixed upon her. His words were those of a courteous host, but in his voice there lurked a touch of irony that was not lost upon her.

Beast! she thought resentfully. Why can't he keep his cat-and-mouse games for the courtroom? You just wait, Mr Barrister, until your mother isn't here and I can tell you exactly what I think of you!

'Delightful,' she murmured.

Mrs Clavell gave her a quick glance. 'You sound a little tired, my dear. We mustn't forget you've had quite a long journey today. Would you like to go up to your room and have a rest until dinner? We shall eat at eight o'clock, if Marie is prompt—which she usually is. And it's all quite informal. Holt has to be bullied into changing for dinner.'

He laid his dark head against the back of the chair. 'My profession demands dressing up, unfortunately,' he said lazily. 'So when I'm here I enjoy throwing off all restraints.'

Again his eyes sought hers and again the message was clear. Avis had had enough of his innuendoes. She got to her feet. 'I'll take your advice and have a rest, Mrs Clavell,' she said. 'I'll bring your papers down later, and then you can go through them at your convenience.' That, she thought, would point up the fact that she was here merely on business and not to provide a convenient lure for a matchmaking mama—or a holiday diversion for her marriage-resistant son.

Up in her room she stripped off her skirt and blouse and lay down on the soft bed. The curtains had been drawn and the room was pleasantly warm. It would be a good idea to sleep until dinner-time and then she might, she hoped, be fresh to meet any challenges. It might also clear her mind about her rather too violent reaction to Holt Clavell. Looked at sanely it was quite clear what had happened. She'd been brooding on the idea of romatic love-at-first-sight ever since Janice had chattered blithely on about the tall dark handsome stranger she was going to meet. Ever since Robert had been so maddeningly prosaic about getting married. It had all been a big joke, but the idea had got into her mind and stayed there. Then, when Holt Clavell suddenly appeared, tall and dark and handsome, leaning nonchalantly against the window frame in the manner of all romantic heroes, her mind had linked him up with the romantic idea already there, and—Wham! Her heart had stood still, just like the song said.

It was the fault of all those old songs that they were always reviving, she thought crossly. 'Some enchanted evening, you may see a stranger——' They were part of a dream world—fascinating so long as you recognised them for what they were. But if you tried to walk into that dream world you did so at your peril. These were times of reality, and Romance with a capital R was *out*.

What she had felt for Holt Clavell had been just body chemistry—lust, if you wanted to be even more precise. He had made it plain that he felt the same way.

And what, Avis Brown, do you intend to do about it?

Resist temptation, the voice of common sense advised. It would be asking for trouble to tangle with a man like him—a man whose job it was to play upon the minds and emotions of witnesses. To coax, to bait, to entice. To reassure blandly and then, when the poor prey was feeling safe, suddenly to move in for the kill. She had been in court with Mr Hanworthy several times, and had watched the barristers in action. She hadn't much liked what she had seen.

No, she thought, working up to a fine state of hostility, I refuse to be a little fish on the end of your line, Mr Clavell. A girl only has to say No, and keep on saying No. It isn't really difficult.

She wished she could dispel the lurking doubt that it might be very difficult indeed.

CHAPTER THREE

AVIS's mouth drooped in disgust as she surveyed the contents of her wardrobe: the darkish brown suit she had travelled in, a couple of unexciting blouses, two simple dresses and her gaberdine mac. She wished now she hadn't been guided in her choice by what she had thought 'suitable' for a secretary to wear on a business trip. So far, this had been very far from a business trip, and looked like going on being so.

But why should she want to look glamorous, for pity's sake? Certainly not to impress Holt Clavell. And yet wouldn't it be safe to dispel the image he must have of her as a naïve little London typist? If she could meet him on his own level she might have a better chance of holding her own against him, and not fall into his arms with glad cries of gratitude the first time he made a serious pass at her—which she was fairly sure he meant to do.

Her heartbeat quickened at the prospect and she gave herself a warning frown in the mirror. 'No, Avis,' she said firmly aloud. 'No fantasising about the man. Forget about the romantic love-at-first-sight fairy story, because that's what it is—a fairy story. The real man, out there in the real world, doesn't want to waste his time following Cinderella round with a satin slipper, to see if it fits. All he wants is to get the girl into bed with him as quickly as possible. And when he gets tired of her, to pass on to the next one.'

Perhaps that wasn't quite fair. Not all men were like that. Robert, for instance, had never propositioned her and he *had* asked her to marry him. But Holt Clavell was a very different type. Holt Clavell was dangerous. He wasn't looking for a wife to bolster his career, as Robert was. Quite the reverse, as he had openly admitted.

So—she had to be very careful with Holt Clavell. She had to plan her defence. And for a start, tomorrow she would go out and buy a really super dress—she had her credit card with her and she was well within her limit. And she would then feel armed to play the part she had chosen. She would act sophisticated even if she wasn't. She would show him that two can put on the ironic, enigmatic air. She would be so confident—so poised——

By the time she went down for dinner she had almost begun to believe it. She swept down the stairs with the gathered skirt of her simple blue dress swinging jauntily round her slender legs. She had taken a long time over her make-up and hoped that the dusky eye-shadow with a sparkle of silver would make up in sophistication what her dress lacked. She had put her hair up in a complicated knot and prayed that it wouldn't fall down again. She was ready to meet Holt's ironic glances with calm self-possession.

So it was something of an anti-climax when Holt hardly looked at her all through dinner. Mrs Clavell's doctor had called in to see her and had been persuaded to stay for a meal. Dr Jago was a darkly good-looking woman in a stylish white tailored suit. She had fine, flashing black eyes, hair as smooth as sealskin and a thin red gash of a mouth. She spoke hardly any English, and after a few halting remarks when Mrs Clavell introduced Avis, she shrugged politely and devoted her attention to Holt.

Holt, it seemed, spoke perfect French. He *would*, Avis thought with rare peevishness. He probably spoke perfect German and Italian and Japanese as well. And Hindustani too. At the other end of the table Mrs Clavell leaned towards her, her eyes resting upon her son with an odd expression in them. 'Dr Jago was involved in treating a bad accident case just recently,' she told Avis in a low voice. 'I expect she's discussing the legal aspects with Holt.'

'Oh yes?' Avis murmured, glancing at the two dark heads so close together and then looking away again quickly. They might be discussing legal aspects, but if they were they found it necessary to laugh together a good deal and Dr Jago's great black eyes were flashing like lighthouse beams.

It was probably an extremely well cooked meal, but Avis was only dimly aware of shrimps and avocado, followed by a succulent chicken dish in a velvety sauce. After that she ceased to notice what she was eating. She must be more tired than she had thought by the journey.

Coffee was served in tiny cups, half full of the strongest brew that Avis had ever tasted. After that Dr Jago took her leave, saying that she had several more calls to make. Holt escorted her to the door and he seemed to Avis to be away an unnecessarily long time.

'Now, let's enjoy some Mozart,' Mrs Clavell said, when they had moved back into the drawing room. 'Put the Clarinet Quintet on, Holt.'

The quality of the hi-fi was superb and the music flowed through the large room like liquid gold. Avis lay back in her chair, deliberately averting her eyes from the man sitting opposite. As the first movement came to an end she raised her head, to see Holt's eyes fixed on her, and her heart gave an uncomfortable jolt. He smiled faintly and jerked his head towards his mother, on the sofa. Avis looked too, and saw that Mrs Clavell was fast asleep. His smile broadened, and it was as if he was offering to share an intimate little family joke with her. She looked away again quickly. It wasn't in her plan to share intimate family jokes with Holt Clavell.

The beautiful slow movement came to an end, the playing arm lifted and the machine switched itself off with a click. Mrs Clavell opened her eyes with a little jerk and blinked apologetically. 'I've been dozing,' she confessed. 'How disgraceful of me, I do apologise to Mozart.' She grinned the little rueful grin that Avis found so attractive. Then suddenly her hand went to her chest and she gave a gasp. She had gone very pale.

Avis was on her feet immediately. 'Are you not feeling well, Mrs Clavell? Can I get you anything?'

It was over in a minute and her hostess was smiling again. 'It's nothing, my dear, thank you. I probably ate too much dinner. I shall take myself off to bed and leave you two young people to enjoy the second side of the record. We'll have it on again tomorrow, perhaps, and I promise to stay awake.'

Holt stood up. 'Is there anything you need, Mama?' His tone was kind but unconcerned. 'Shall I bring you up a warm drink?'

'No, thank you, dear. I shall lie in bed and listen to the rest of the music from a distance. My bedroom is just overhead,' she added to Avis.

Holt went over and opened the door. 'Goodnight, children,' Mrs Clavell included them both in her smile and went out.

Holt went back to the hi-fi, turned the record

over and set the mechanism. As the sound of the
minuet filled the room he went across to a built-in
drinks cabinet and opened the doors.

'What's your fancy?' he asked Avis over his
shoulder. 'We're fairly well stocked.' He waved a
hand towards the sparkling array of bottles and
glasses.

Avis was on the point of refusing anything and
following her hostess out of the room. Then she
remembered that she was supposed to be poised
and self-confident. 'Something long and cool,
please,' she said. 'Lime juice would be lovely.' She
tried to put the faintest drawl into her voice.

He looked round, and she met his eyes without
flinching. 'And——?' her quieried, holding up a tall
glass with ice clinking in the pale yellow liquid
inside.

'Oh——' She appeared to consider. 'Gin?'

'Certainly, *mademoiselle*.' He carried the glass
across and set it down on the low table next to the
sofa. Then he set his own brandy glass beside it,
relaxed into the cushioned sofa and patted the
place beside him.

'Come and listen to Mozart with me,' he invited
lazily.

She smiled sweetly. 'I'm very comfortable where
I am, thanks.'

Holt raised an eyebrow, shrugged slightly, laid
his head back and closed his eyes.

It was the first time in her life that Avis didn't
give her full attention to a Mozart piece. All her
senses were tinglingly occupied with the man on
the sofa. She was aware of him as she had never
been aware of any man before—in a completely
different way. She couldn't believe she had only
met him a few hours ago, and that she knew
hardly anything about him. She watched him

under her lashes and marvelled at his stillness, at his complete lack of any nervous twitches, even the tiniest movement of his fingers. He was like a great cat, she thought. A leopard, or a tiger. He had the gift of complete relaxation as he lay back on the sofa, long legs in front of him crossed at the ankle, thick dark lashes resting on his cheeks. Even in the short interval of silence before the final movement started he didn't move a muscle. But when the record finally came to an end he opened his eyes and looked straight into hers. She had the feeling that he had been watching her all the time and her heart started to thump uncomfortably.

The hi-fi switched itself off and the silence in the room was complete. Avis swallowed hard, her throat as dry as chaff. This was when she should make some remark—say something light and assured, something appreciative of the music, perhaps. But she couldn't say a word. The long meeting of eyes was having a hypnotic effect on her and when he finally—still without speaking— slowly and deliberately held out a hand to her, it was as if she was drawn towards him by a force over which she had no control.

A moment later she found herself on the sofa beside him. His arm was round her and he was drawing her head against his shoulder.

'That's better,' he said. 'Much more friendly!' He pressed his cheek against the top of her head.

'Well,' he went on in a conversational tone, 'you've seen how it is with Mama. Can you doubt that I was telling you the truth?'

'I really haven't considered the matter particularly,' she said composedly, trying to ignore the wild thumping of her heart. She moved her shoulders to shrug, but his hand was restraining them. The pressure of his fingers made her yearn to snuggle further into his arms. It took a real effort to restrain herself.

'Little liar,' he said softly.

'How dare you?' It was difficult to be suitably indignant when every nerve in her body was tingling. She made a weak effort to draw away but he pulled her back into his arms.

'Oh, I dare,' he said. 'Didn't I tell you it's my job to know when people are telling the truth? It's all too rare.'

'What a beastly cynical thing to say!'

He laughed and rubbed his cheek against hers. 'It's my experience, nevertheless. And it would be a very uncomfortable world if we all told the truth to each other all the time, don't you think?'

His head had turned while he was talking and now his mouth was moving from her ear down to her chin.

'I d-don't know,' Avis stammered.

'For instance,' he murmured, 'what would you say if I asked whether you want me as much as I want you—now, this minute?'

The shock ran all through her body, robbing her of speech. Then she drew a quivering breath. 'I'd say—I'd say you're insulting, Mr Clavell, if you think for a moment that I'm a girl who——' she gulped humiliatingly '—who gives herself to any man she's just met, just because he—he——'

'Yes?' he said quietly. His hand came up and turned her face towards him and he looked searchingly into her eyes. 'He what?'

'He knows how to—to turn a girl on,' she muttered helplessly.

His dark lashes dropped lower. 'So you admit I turn you on?'

She wriggled wildly in his grasp. 'What sort of a game are you playing, Mr Clavell? Please let me go.'

'Not until you've answered my question—truthfully. And don't you think you might call me Holt, as we're going to know each other much better as the week goes on.'

She went on wriggling and he held her quite loosely but made it impossible for her to get out of his grasp. 'All right,' she said desperately, 'as you're so very clever you must know quite well that you turn me on. You've learned your technique from vast experience, I suppose.' She tried to sound dignified, but the words came out merely childish.

'We-ell,' he drawled, 'we've established that I can give you twelve years at the least. I've had a certain amount of free time in that period when I needed relaxation from my work. One picks up a few hints here and there about what pleases a woman.' He chuckled softly. 'Let me demonstrate.'

His mouth closed over hers and her struggling stopped as a warm tide of desire washed over her. His kiss was like no other kiss she had ever had before, and she realised dimly for the first time that every man's kiss is somehow unique. After the first moment she found herself responding intuitively, her mouth moving against his, following where he led, and as his hand unbuttoned the front of her dress and closed over her breast she shuddered and pressed closer against him, her arms going up round his neck, her fingers tangling in his thick hair.

Holt drew his head back at last and in the subdued lighting his eyes glittered like jet. 'I think,' he said quite calmly, 'that I've established the truth, haven't I?'

Avis put a hand to her wildly dishevelled head. The fashionable knot that she had taken so much trouble over had come loose and strands of silky brown hair hung across her cheeks and tickled her neck. He reached round and pulled the last two pins out and the whole silken mass came free and cascaded round her face. 'I like it better that way,' he said. 'Why did you put it up? To look older than you are? That's usually a mistake, Avis.' He was laughing at her. The kisses that had shaken her to the core had meant little or nothing to him, of course. To him she was still a naïve little London typist, good for a kiss and a cuddle, but not expected to be capable of meeting him on his own level—intellectually or in any other way.

She stood up, willing her legs to support her. 'Goodnight, Mr Clavell,' she said coldly. 'You've proved your point, so please don't feel it necessary to repeat the performance.'

'Didn't you enjoy it? I thought you seemed to.'

She had control of herself now. 'That's nothing to do with it. I enjoy chocolate éclairs, but I don't gorge myself on them, because I know I would despise myself afterwards.'

He gave a hoot of laughter. 'You have a picturesque turn of phrase, Miss Brown. I think we're going to get on very well.'

Avis lifted her chin. 'I doubt if we shall see very much of each other, Mr Clavell,' she said coolly. 'I understand you're working on a brief and I shall no doubt be busy carrying out your mother's wishes.'

When she saw his eyebrows lift she realised too late the full implication of what she had just said. He chuckled. 'If that's your plan, my girl, then I imagine we shall see a *great* deal of each other.'

'Oh, you—you——' she burst out in helpless rage.

At that moment came the sound of knocking on the floor of the room overhead. 'Mama,' said

Holt, and stood up. 'She probably can't wait to find out how we're getting on together. I'll go up and set her mind at rest.'

He was back before Avis could escape up to her room. 'It's you that Mama wants to see,' he said. 'Would you mind going up? It's the door at the end of the passage.'

Avis ran upstairs and into her own room. Here she quickly combed her hair and pinned it up again, hoping that her hostess wouldn't notice that the result was far from immaculate. Then she went along the passage and tapped at the door at the end. Mrs Clavell was lying back against lace-trimmed pillows. She wore a fleecy white bedjacket and she looked pale and beautiful and very frail in the middle of the big bed.

Avis walked across the shadowy room, lit only by the bedside lamp, and stood beside the bed. 'How are you, Mrs Clavell—are you feeling better?'

'A little, thank you, my dear, but not really very good, I must admit.' Avis thought that the fine grey eyes had a frightened look. 'I mustn't complain, though. Holt says I worry too much about myself, and maybe he's right.' She sighed. 'But sometimes I wonder——' She smiled wryly. 'There I am, off again! I'm just a foolish old woman. I'll be fine in the morning.'

'I'm sure you're not foolish,' Avis said quietly. 'Now, let me get you a warm drink before you settle off to sleep. I always used to do that for my mother if she was feeling a bit under the weather. What would you like? Shall I find Marie and ask her?'

'Marie and Jacques will most likely have gone home by now,' Mrs Clavell said. 'They have a little house down in Menton, in the old town.'

'Well, I'm sure I can find something if I look around in the kitchen,' Avis said. 'Warm milk—Horlicks—Ovaltine?'

'It's very good of you, my dear, you're a kind girl. I must admit to enjoying a cup of tea last thing. I know it's supposed to be stimulating, but it seems to make me feel better and then I drop off to sleep more easily.'

'Right,' said Avis promptly, 'tea it shall be. I'll rummage round and find everything. Shan't be long.' She took the memory of Mrs Clavell's rather pathetically grateful smile downstairs with her. She certainly needs a daughter, Avis thought. Holt isn't exactly the soul of sympathy—I can just hear him saying, 'Stop thinking about yourself so much, Mama.' So like a man!

The kitchen was easily found. It was smallish and beautifully fitted in panelled wood, and Marie had left everything clean and neat. Avis put the kettle on to boil, set cups and saucers on a tray and took a canister of Earl Grey tea from the selection in the cupboard. She opened some more cupboard doors and found a tin of digestive biscuits and added that to the tray, with a jug of milk from the fridge.

Holt appeared in the doorway as the kettle was coming to the boil. His dark brows lifted ironically. 'Quite the little housewife, aren't you?'

'Any objection?' Avis enquired coldly. 'Your mother said she would enjoy a cup of tea, so I'm making one, that's all. There doesn't seem anyone else to look after her.'

He leaned against the doorpost eyeing her calmly. 'Do I detect a note of criticism?'

Avis poured the boiling water into the teapot. 'Detect what you please,' she said tartly.

She put the teapot on the tray, but before

picking it up she hesitated. 'Mr Clavell——' she began.

'Holt,' he said smoothly.

In her urge to find words for what she wanted to say she forgot to feel embarrassed at calling him by his name. 'Holt, then,' she said, almost impatiently. 'Do you think—I mean, are you sure——' She broke off, biting her lip.

His brows lifted slightly. 'Take your time.'

The amused note in his voice annoyed her sufficiently to make her forget her diffidence. 'Are you quite sure,' she went on, choosing her words carefully, 'that your mother isn't rather more unwell than you seem to believe? I thought she looked wretched when I saw her a few minutes ago.'

His smile pulled down the corners of his mouth. 'I see you've fallen under the spell of my fascinating mama,' he said. 'My dear girl, she's been playing that little game for years—ever since my father died, in fact. He adored her and spoilt her hopelessly, and she's never really come to terms with the fact that she must stand on her own two feet now and that she should have many years of active life ahead of her. Dr Jago says there's nothing at all wrong with her. She prescribes some pills now and again—placebos, probably, which are made of sugar, I believe, and tells her to rest. And that's about all she can do. The very worst thing you can do for people who play for sympathy, my child, is to give it to them, so be warned.'

Avis still hesitated, holding the tray. To her Mrs Clavell looked so frail that it seemed brutal to treat her so casually. 'I suppose you're right and it's none of my business, but I'm still not quite convinced.' She met his eyes and, greatly

daring, said, 'You have confidence in Dr Jago's
opinion?'

His expression changed, his mouth hardened.
'As you say, it's none of your business, Miss
Brown,' he said curtly. 'Now, go up and get on
with your tea and sympathy—and don't forget my
warning.' He turned and walked away.

Avis found she was trembling with annoyance as
she carried the tray upstairs. Was this the cold, legal
mind she had heard so much about? If so, she didn't
care for it at all. He was callous—almost inhuman!
And she wouldn't trust that Dr Jago's opinion for a
moment. She wouldn't like to have *her* for a doctor if
she were ill; there wasn't a bit of warmth in those
glittering black eyes and that straight, clever mouth.
She and Holt Clavell would make a good pair—and
good luck to the two of them!

And if Holt tried any of his fascinating tricks on
her—Avis—again she would jolly well know how
to deal with him! Her cheeks were pink as she
carried the tray into Mrs Clavell's room.

When she left it, half an hour later, she felt a
glow of satisfied certainty that Holt was quite
wrong. There had been no bid for sympathy, and
her hostess had seemed quite animated and
pleased to have someone to chat to. 'You bring a
little spring into the house, Avis,' she had smiled,
'so please don't insist upon my going through my
papers too quickly, for then you'll have to go back
to London. Have a few days' holiday—I'm sure
you've been working hard through the worst of the
winter and deserve it. You must take a look at our
famous local festival. The processions take place
on Sunday.'

'Oh yes, the Fête du Citron. I'd like that,' said
Avis. 'Jacques was telling me about it.'

Mrs Clavell nodded. 'It's one of the best. We

have an assortment of festivals and celebrations along the Coast all through the year—every place has its own attraction. There's the Mimosa Festival in Cannes and the quite fantastic carnival in Nice. There are film festivals and jazz festivals and all the wine harvest festivals at the end of the season. But I think the Lemon Festival in Menton is one of the prettiest. Everything is decorated with oranges and lemons—it's quite amazing what they do with them—*and* how many they waste, I'm afraid. But it's all very jolly and there's a lighthearted atmosphere in the place. My husband and I always went down into the town at festival time.' She added with a tender smile, 'He was one of the eternal young-at-heart.'

Not like his son, Avis thought, and said, 'Holt did mention the festival, but he said he always avoided it, it was so crowded.'

His mother smiled tolerantly. 'That sounds like Holt! Sometimes these legal men forget how to play. But if he feels like that about it we'll find some nice young man to take you, Avis. You just leave it to me.'

Avis remembered that remark as she undressed in her pretty white room. Surely if Mrs Clavell was trying to use her as bait to get Holt married she wouldn't be arranging for her to be escorted by some other young man? Avis yawned hugely and snuggled down in bed. She was too tired to try to work it out now. It had been quite a day since she got on the plane at Heathrow early this morning. A lot had happened. She had come to the fabulous French Riviera for the first time, and fallen in love with the place.

It's quite safe to fall in love with a *place*, she thought sleepily. Just see that it stays that way, Avis.

Mrs Clavell was as good as her word. Before lunch next day Avis had met an extremely good-looking young Frenchman called Pierre, who, from the start, did not try to hide his admiration.

She had breakfasted in bed—an almost unknown luxury—visited Mrs Clavell in her room where she had once again been put off about producing the legal documents, and drifted downstairs into the drawing room. There was no sign of Holt and Avis presumed that he was closeted away working on his brief. That, she told herself, was a relief. Everywhere was tidy and polished. Marie must have been about her work at an early hour. The room looked beautiful, so it must be just her imagination that it had a dull, lifeless feeling about it. It couldn't have been due to the fact that Holt wasn't here, could it?

The door on to the veranda was open and Avis walked out and stood leaning on the wooden rail, looking down towards the streak of blue water in the far distance. Immediately below the veranda the garden fell away in uneven layers of terraces where plants and shrubs rioted wildly. To her left, a walled bed of enormous cacti spread out their spiky, prickly leaves, looking amusingly similar to their tiny relatives on the kitchen windowsill at home, only gigantically larger. The branches of a mimosa tree overhung the bed, thick with fluffy yellow blossom, and the scent of it filled the morning air. The sunshine seemed to be getting warmer with every passing moment.

February! Avis thought once again, remembering the cold and wet of London. How incredibly lucky she was to be here! If only she could enjoy it in a carefree sort of way without this love-hate relationship that had developed with Holt Clavell.

It complicated everything and spoilt everything. In spite of the glorious morning she began to feel vaguely depressed.

Suddenly she was aware that someone was standing behind her and she caught her breath. Holt! She spun round, the blood rushing to her cheeks. But it wasn't Holt. A young man of about her own age stood there, smiling. Polished dark hair, neatly parted; sloe-dark eyes on an olive skin; a thin, boyish figure; he was almost certainly French.

'Mademoiselle Avis? *Bonjour, mademoiselle. Je suis enchanté,'* he said with formal politeness, and then added, in English, 'Madame Clavell 'as telephoned my mother and suggested that I call, Pierre Taudevin at your service.' He gave a little bow. He was really very good-looking.

Avis held out her hand, returning his smile. 'I'm afraid Madame is not up yet.'

He took her hand and held it with an air of gallantry. 'Ah, but it is not Madame Clavell I come to see—it is you, *mademoiselle.* Madame Clavell has explained to my *maman* that you stay here at present and that she wishes for an escort for you to our Fête du Citron. I come to ask if you will allow me the honour of accompanying you.'

The wicked gleam in his dancing dark eyes contradicted the formality of his words, and Avis began to feel more cheerful. She'd got her romantic heroes mixed up. *This* young man was the dark handsome stranger that Janice had promised she would meet on her short trip into the playground of the beautiful people—not the arrogant, calculating Holt Clavell, who had such a devastating pull on her emotions.

'Thank you, I'd be delighted,' she said, bubbling with relief. 'It all sounds tremendous fun.'

'It will be fun, I promise you,' he said. 'Already my *maman* has two seats for the stand to see the procession, but she has received a call from my aunt in Paris to visit her, so she hopes you will accept her ticket.'

They sat together on the veranda in the sunshine and Avis said how marvellous it was to be able to sit out of doors in February, and soon they were talking in a friendly way about their jobs. Pierre worked with his father in a photographic business in Menton, but he had ambitions to become a freelance journalistic photographer.

'I shall take many pictures of the Fête,' he said. 'You will not be too bored?'

'Of course not,' Avis laughed. 'So long as you send me one when I get home, to remind me of Menton.'

'But certainly. I shall also take many pictures of the most beautiful girl at the Fête—to remind *me*.' His dark eyes twinkled down at her. 'But now, alas, duty calls and I must say *au revoir*, Mademoiselle Avis. I shall call for you on Sunday, yes?'

Avis felt quite elated when Pierre had gone. She went up to Mrs Clavell's room and tapped at the door. Her hostess was sitting up in bed with the photograph album on her knee. She was wearing a lacy white wrap and Avis thought she looked even more fragile in the morning light than she had looked last night.

But she smiled delightfully when she saw Avis. 'Good morning, dear, did you sleep well, and have you got over your travel-tiredness? I'm very lazy in the mornings, as you can see. I've been brooding on my old photographs again—getting dangerously nostalgic, I'm afraid!' There was a glint of tears behind the smiling grey eyes as she closed the album. 'Oh, I must warn you, by the way, you may be receiving a visit from a delightful young man—the son of a friend of mine—called Pierre Taudevin. He——'

'Yes. I've met him already, that's what I came to tell you, Mrs Clavell. Pierre called in a short while ago and introduced himself, and he's invited me to go to the Fête with him. His mother had a seat booked in the stand to see the procession, but she can't go, so I'm to have her ticket. I'm very thrilled and I wanted to say how grateful I am to you for arranging it.'

'Not at all, Avis. I think it's a splendid idea.' She chuckled as if she were enjoying some private joke. 'I'm very pleased too.'

'I wondered——' Avis, began, 'perhaps I could go down into the town some time today? I should like to buy a dress to wear at the Fête. I brought only what I thought suitable for a secretary to wear, but you've been so kind and made me almost a guest, Mrs Clavell——'

'My dear child, you *are* a guest,' Mrs Clavell assured her, 'and a very delightful one, too. I'm sure you'll look charming in whatever you choose to wear, but I can quite understand that you'd like to buy something light and festive. Jacques is doing the garden today, you'll find him out there somewhere. Tell him I said he was to drive you into the town and wait to bring you back. Holt is immersed in his work, otherwise I'm sure he would have liked to take you himself.' It seemed to Avis that Mrs Clavell's eyes were fixed rather keenly upon her as she said that.

Avis thanked her. 'I was going to ask where I could get a taxi——' she began, but Mrs Clavell wouldn't hear of it.

'Go and buy something pretty and come and

show it to me when you get back—I used to adore buying pretty clothes, but now I have to admire them on someone young,' she added with her rueful little smile. 'Have you brought enough francs with you?'

'I have a credit card,' Avis explained. 'I thought I'd use that.'

Mrs Clavell reached to the bedside table for a pad and pencil. 'Try this shop,' she said. 'I'm sure you'll find what you want there. And if you tell them you're staying with me they'll look after you. Now, go along and enjoy yourself.' Her smile was warm and she gave Avis's hand a little pat, but there was a wistful look in her grey eyes.

Avis found that shopping in Menton was rather alarming. She stood outside the shop mentioned by Mrs Clavell and did mental sums, converting the francs into pounds. The result staggered her. After that she wandered round, looking in the windows of other glossy establishments, but they all seemed terrifyingly expensive. Menton was indeed a millionaire's playground—no budget holiday here!

But she had made up her mind to buy a dress to wear tomorrow, so she took a deep breath and pushed open the heavy glass doors of the boutique that Mrs Clavell had recommended. Avis was accustomed to fighting her way through the big Oxford Street stores in London, and the muted luxury of this exclusive establishment gave her butterflies in the tummy.

A vendeuse glided up to her, terrifyingly chic in a black dress that fitted like a skin. Avis thought, goodness, I hope I have a figure that like when I'm pushing forty!

The woman took a quick look at Avis and said, in English, 'Can I help Mademoiselle?'

Avis was amazed. 'You knew I was English?'

'But certainly, *mademoiselle*. Your so-exquisite complexion announces the fact.'

Well, that was a confidence-booster. Avis grinned and thanked her, and from that moment on they were friends and allies, both intent upon the one matter of importance at the moment, that of selecting a dress that would transform Avis from a secretary on a business trip into a stylish young woman taking a holiday on the Côte d'Azur.

'That is the one, do you not agree?' the vendeuse announced at last, when Avis was feeling positively dizzy with the wealth of beautiful dresses that she had tried on. 'That suits Mademoiselle—but *parfaitement*.' She eased the skirt over Avis's slender hips. 'It is so romantic, do you not think?'

Avis twirled in front of the long mirror. The subtly-gathered skirt the colour of Devonshire cream, the wispy blouse of paler cream with a shell-pink stripe and a lace-trimmed button-band; the swingy little jacket and pink leather tie-sash. It was perfect. And romantic—oh yes, it was romantic too. It asked for what Janice had called 'Little restaurants hidden away among the palm trees.' It seemed to fit in with the promise of Pierre Taudevin's dancing dark eyes that had turned on her with such admiration.

Yes, Avis said, doing reckless sums in her head, she would have it. *And* the cream and pink striped cotton blazer, because, as the vendeuse told her, the evenings could get very cool at this time of the year. Cream sandals and a small cream shoulder-bag completed the outfit.

She left the establishment feeling the bubbling excitement that a new dress can give to any girl.

Thank heaven for Pierre, she thought—he was just perfect for a holiday flirtation. Tall, dark and handsome, but with none of Holt Clavell's smouldering charisma. He was like a sparkling light wine, compared with a devil's brew that knocked you silly after the first sip.

'I took one look at you——' she carolled under her breath, as she walked briskly along the wide, smooth pavement with the breeze on her cheeks and the sunlight turning the sea to silver. The trouble was that she had happened to look at the wrong man first. It was funny, when you came to think of it. She giggled as she went to find Jacques in the car park. There was an air of expectancy about the whole of Menton today. On the way she passed the beginnings of the Fête—enormous set-pieces made from dozens and dozens of small lemons and oranges. One was in the shape of the Eiffel Tower, another was a great camel. Everywhere was being decorated with the sunshine-yellow of the fruit.

Oh, it was going to be fun. Avis thought. She was glad, glad, glad that Holt Clavell was too beastly superior to join in. She wouldn't have any fun with *him*. As she saw Jacques leaning against the car she waved and broke into a little skipping run. She couldn't wait for tomorrow.

CHAPTER FOUR

HOLT was standing in the front doorway when Jacques pulled the car up. He didn't move, just stood there leaning against the doorpost, arrogant as ever. Avis's heart gave a jolt and started thumping away like mad. It was humiliating, her immediate physical response to this man, just when she had thought she was getting him out of her system. But she ignored it and waited for Jacques to come round and open the car door for her, before she gathered up her handbag and the boxes and carriers and climbed out, with as much dignity as possible. It wasn't easy to emerge from a car clutching numerous parcels and still remain poised. Especially when *that man* was standing there observing her lazily under those hooded eyelids.

'Morning, Avis. Up and out with the lark, I see,' he said chattily. He looked at the dress boxes. 'Lovely morning for a shopping spree.'

'Good morning, Mr Clavell.' Avis spoke as dismissively as she could, short of being deliberately rude. Seeing him standing there had quite marred the feeling of euphoria she had had in Menton. She must show him in no uncertain way that the episode of last night was not to be repeated. She climbed the last few steps to the front door looking straight ahead, with her chin in the air. It rather spoilt the effect when the ribbon round one of the boxes came untied and the box dropped to the top step. Holt picked it up and handed it back.

'Thank you,' she said, and as he made no move to get out of the doorway, 'May I pass, please?'

He stood aside with a mocking little bow, and followed her into the hall. 'Avis—one moment, please,' he said, as she put a foot on the bottom stair.

She turned but didn't walk back to him. 'Yes, Mr Clavell?'

'I have a favour to ask of you. You may decline if you wish, but I think it would please Mama if you agreed. It was, of course, her idea.'

She waited in silence for him to go on.

'Nothing that will stretch your talents, I'm sure. It's just that I have a lot of paper-work to get through today and it would be a great help if you could spare an hour or two to type out some notes for me. Do say No if you'd rather not,' he added with what she thought was rather excessive politeness.

Avis knew she should say No. She had determined on evasive action where Holt Clavell was concerned and now he was asking her to work with him, to be in his company for hours at a time probably. It was maddening. And yet—and yet——

'Yes, of course I'll help, if I can,' she heard herself say.

'Good girl,' he said. 'I'm very grateful. Right after lunch in my study—O.K.?'

She was only going to do some typing, and yet she felt as if she'd been invited to Buckingham Palace.

Holt's study was a cubbyhole of a room at the back of the house, furnished with a huge table and very little else. The villa was built into the hillside, and in this room the rocks, with shrubs clinging to them, rose up almost vertically outside the window.

'It's a bit dark in here,' said Holt, switching on a

daylight strip lamp in the ceiling. 'I chose this room to keep for my work when I'm here so that I can't get distracted looking at the view.' He pulled out a chair in front of a portable typewriter. 'Think you can manage with this machine? It's not exactly space-age technology, but I only use it for notes. Will that chair do you? I can find a cushion if it's too low.'

Avis sat down. 'It's quite O.K., thanks.' He really was being extraordinarily anxious to make her comfortable. He must be desperate for some help.

He rolled up the sleeves of his white shirt and pulled a sheaf of papers from his briefcase. 'This is what I want—if you can make out my awful scrawl.' He pushed the papers across the table to her and came round and stood behind her. There was hardly room between the back of her chair and the wall and he had to stand very close. *Too* close. Avis felt her throat contract and her heart begin to thump. This was crazy, she thought uneasily, she should never have agreed to come. The cell-like room had a dangerous intimacy.

She sat scarcely breathing, sure that his arms were going to close round her, longing for it to happen with a longing so intense that it shocked her.

'From here, on page two——' His finger pointed. His bare arm was only inches away from the soft swell of her breast under her thin blouse. She sat rigid, her heart hammering so hard that it seemed impossible that he shouldn't hear it. She could see the dark hairs that ran from his wrist up his forearm. She could smell the faintly astringent smell of the cologne he used. It took every ounce of strength she possessed not to turn and meet his eyes, to invite a caress.

'—to about here.' The sheets rustled as he flicked them over. His voice was curiously husky.

'Yes,' Avis whispered, sitting very still.

For perhaps thirty seconds they remained still as statues, then Holt moved away abruptly, with a sigh. 'I'll leave you to it, then,' he said. 'Ask me if you get stuck.' The next moment she heard the door close behind him.

When the room was empty she sat staring at the typewriter and wondering if she could go on kidding herself any longer that she wasn't crazily in love with Holt Clavell. And 'crazily' was the operative word. There was no future in falling for Holt—a man who would take a girl merely as relaxation from his work, as he had admitted himself. Oh, why wasn't I like Janice, she thought miserably, instead of being (as she was beginning to suspect) something so unfashionable as a one-man girl?

She pushed back her hair and drew the sheaf of notes towards her. Even his scribbled handwriting, firm and black, garnished with arrows and bubbles and crossings-out, had the power to tie her inside up in knots. She wondered if she could keep a page to hide away in a drawer and look at sometimes, when she had left and wouldn't see him again. Or perhaps she *would* see him, if she went to court with Mr Hanworthy. Holt would look quite magnificent in a gown and wig, she thought fatuously. 'Come on, Avis, snap out of it,' she said aloud, and began to transcribe the notes.

It was after three o'clock by the time she finished. Holt himself hadn't appeared again, and she wondered what she would have done if she *had* got stuck. But the transcribing of the notes had presented little difficulty, and her experience with Mr Hanworthy had helped. She got quite interested in the case as she went on, although she couldn't understand all the complex details. It seemed that some man called Williamson, the chief cashier of a large company that had gone bankrupt, was being accused of theft by falsifying the company's books and stealing large sums of money. Holt was defending the cashier. It was a complicated case, involving masses of figures— profit-and-loss accounts, balance sheets, reports, and thick wads of computer data. As she typed the notes Avis could well understand why Holt had had to work far into the night assembling the evidence, all of which was ranged against the directors of the company. She gathered that his case was that they were making the cashier a scapegoat to save themselves from having to pay out huge sums of compensation to their employees and shareholders. Avis found herself on the cashier's side and hoped fervently that Holt would get him off. She piled up the pages of typescript neatly and placed them on Holt's side of the desk. Then she went up to her room and swilled her face and took a lot of care over her make-up and her hair, so that when Mrs Clavell told her that Holt had gone out and probably wouldn't be back until late this evening, it seemed rather a waste.

'He's driven into the town to see Dr Jago, and pick up a prescription for me,' Mrs Clavell settled down on her sofa beside the tea-table. 'And he's taking her out for dinner, I understand. She has to give evidence in some accident case and she seems to be relying on Holt's advice.' Mrs Clavell gave a quick, sideways glance at Avis and added, 'A handsome young woman, didn't you think? Holt and Hélène Jago see a good deal of each other.' She sighed. 'I wouldn't want *two* daughters-in-law who would be a disappointment to me. One is quite enough! But I'm talking too much, aren't I—and I mustn't bore you with my family problems.'

Avis gulped her tea, which was too hot and scalded her mouth. Holt—and the Jago woman! She felt quite sick as a wave of pure green jealousy washed over her. Mrs Clavell was looking rather hard at her and she had to force herself to mumble something trite to the effect that all families have their problems.

For some reason Mrs Clavell suddenly looked much more cheerful. 'So you and I will have to keep each other company, my dear,' she said. 'That will be very pleasant. We will have a little dinner together and then, perhaps, listen to some more Mozart. And you must get a good night's sleep as you're having a day out with that nice young Pierre tomorrow. Did you find yourself a pretty dress this morning? Do go and put it on after tea and show it to me, and then I can think of you having a lovely day and charming that young man, as I'm sure you will.'

Avis wakened next morning with the sunlight streaming into her bedroom, the birds singing outside her window, and a black lump of depression somewhere in the region of her chest. She toyed with the breakfast tray that Marie brought up, showered, and sat in front of the dressing table mirror trying to recapture the feeling of pleasant anticipation that she had had yesterday—before Holt had left her to cope with the typing work and gone off to see Hélène Jago.

But by the time she had dressed in her new pink and white outfit and brushed her hair into a silky sheen, she had begun to feel cheerful again, and when Marie came in to say that Mrs Clavell was resting this morning, but hoped Mademoiselle would have a nice day, and that Monsieur Taudevin had arrived and was waiting outside in his car for her, she had managed to pin an expectant smile on her mouth, even if her sherry-brown eyes lacked their customary sparkle.

She ran downstairs, praying that she wouldn't encounter Holt, but there was no sign of him. For a second the thought crossed her mind that he might have spent the night with Hélène Jago, and she pressed a hand to her breast. The corny old saying about jealousy being like a knife turning in your heart was true, then. She'd never encountered it before and she hoped fervently that it wouldn't last long. It was agony.

Pierre beamed at her from the driving seat of a very smart white coupé. He vaulted over the door and came round to greet her, French fashion, with a kiss on both cheeks.

He took her hands and held her away from him admiringly. 'But you look—how do you say it in English?—out of this world, Mademoiselle Avis. I am very honoured that you will come out with me.'

'Thank you, Pierre. You're looking very smart yourself.' He looked extremely handsome this morning, in black jeans a blouson jacket in soft beige suede, with a cream silk shirt. His hair gleamed like patent leather and his teeth were white against his Mediterranean tan. A young man any girl would be happy to spend a day with. Avis climbed into the car beside him and as they drove away she resisted the temptation to take a backward look towards the house.

'There will be no space to park in the town,' he told her. 'I shall put my car in our own home, and we shall walk from there, *oui*?'

Pierre's home was a large opulent-looking house

on the outskirts of Menton, and he parked the car in the front drive and then they walked into the town. Avis found her spirits rising as they mingled with the crowd on the promenade. It seemed that more and more people were piling in every minute, and Pierre took her arm to steer her along. 'We will get to our seats in the stand before the first procession comes along,' he said, slinging his camera more firmly over his shoulder. He leaned towards her, pressing her arm, his white smile flashing in the sunshine. 'I have the prettiest girl in Menton as a partner,' he said, close to her ear. 'The prettiest girl in the whole of France!'

Avis laughed at this absurdity, but it set the tone for the day. Pierre was extravagantly admiring. He hung on her words, laughed at her small jokes. Avis was sure that he would have put on the same polished performance for the benefit of any girl he escorted.

Their seats in the stand were next to those of two friends of Pierre's, whom he introduced to Avis as Edouard and Louise. Edouard was a lanky young man with an infectious grin, and Louise petite, with huge, sad eyes that turned adoringly upon Edouard every few moments.

'They are very much in love,' Pierre confided into Avis's ear, 'they would marry if there was enough money, but——' he lifted the palms of his hands in a descriptive gesture. 'Perhaps,' he added with a wry twist to his mouth, 'it is better so. They are both very young. One does not know one's mind, as they say, when one falls in love too young.'

Avis laughed. 'You're a philosopher, Pierre.'

'No, no,' he denied it. 'I have the common sense, that is all. One should not take the great falling in love too seriously, but one does, and then one is unhappy. Ah, but the romance, that is different. It is——' he sighed and slipped an arm round her waist as they sat close together on the wooden seats '—it is—*merveilleux*, do you not agree, Mademoiselle Avis? It is to be enjoyed for as long as it lasts.'

The great falling in love, as the practical Pierre put it, and the fleeting romance—they should not be confused. A picture of Holt Clavell's thin, clever face, of the hooded magnetic eyes and the sensual line of his mouth appeared for a moment before her eyes, and her inside felt hollow. What was it that drew her magnetically to him—love— or romance—or just plain sex? She didn't know and she pushed the thought away. She wasn't going to let her foolishness spoil this lovely day. The sun was shining out of a cloudless blue sky. The waves were creaming on to the pale fringe of sand. The crowds on the promenade, under the tall palm trees, were in festive mood, and more people were pouring into the town every moment. Somewhere a band was playing—two bands, vying with each other for hearers' attention.

She smiled into Pierre's dancing dark eyes. 'I think you're right,' she said. Romance was to be enjoyed—and forgotten.

The day of the Fête du Citron was pure romance. For Avis everything was new and exhilarating. She watched, fascinated, the procession of what Pierre called the *Fruits d'Or* (which he translated for her as the golden fruits). She had seen processions before, of course, May Day processions in the Midlands town where she had grown up with her mother, but this one was different. All the great set-pieces were made up entirely of thousands and thousands of lemons, with oranges to provide contrast. As the great

floats came trundling slowly along there were
gasps of admiration from the crowds and clapping
and shouting, and plenty of jokes passing
backwards and forwards from the pretty girls in
folk costume riding on the wagons.

Avis was entranced. 'Oh, look, Pierre!' she
squealed as yet another great yellow and orange
masterpiece came into view. 'This one is all the
Signs of the Zodiac. Mine is Taurus—do look at
that wonderful Bull! What's your sign, Pierre?'

'My sign is Gemini,' he told her, laughing into
her eyes. 'One lovely lady isn't enough for me, you
see. I have two.' He pointed to the twins, hand-in-
hand, with their orange dresses and their lemon
hair.

The procession seemed to take hours—the great
floats passing slowly with their different themes.
Of music, of fishing, of country people. One was
of Adam and Eve, and Pierre explained the local
legend to Avis, as best he could, over all the
noise of the singing and the bands playing. When
Adam and Eve were expelled from Paradise, he
said, Eve stole a lemon and hid it in her hair.
When they reached Menton she was so over-
whelmed by the beauty of the place that she threw
down the lemon, saying 'Grow and multiply,' and
soon the slopes of the hills nearby were covered
with golden fruit.

Finally the procession had passed and then
Pierre devoted himself to his photography. With
Edouard and Louise they mingled with the crowds
on the sea-front; they watched side-shows; they
bought ice-creams, which were deliciously different from any ice-creams that Avis had ever tasted
in England. They stopped at a small café and
drank coffee and ate spicy biscuits, and Pierre
went on photographing everything within range.

'He is—how you say?—obsess with his camera,' Edouard confided to Avis. 'Some day he will be a famous photographer.'

But at last the sun began to go down and there was a chill in the air and the crowds thinned out. 'I think, perhaps, I should be getting back to Madame Clavell's house,' Avis said to Pierre, who was fiddling with the exposure meter of his camera.

He stopped fiddling immediately and pulled a horrified face at her. 'Go back so soon? But no, *ma chérie*, you cannot do that to me! I have arranged with Edouard that we all eat at a restaurant and then we go back to my home. My parents are away tonight, but they would not object at all, I promise you. We can put on music and dance, perhaps. I wish very much that you accompany us. I shall be heartbroken if you leave me so soon.' He squeezed her hand and gazed soulfully into her eyes. 'You do not wish to return so soon?'

'Well—no, of course not,' Avis admitted. She was enjoying her day and she didn't want it to finish. Certainly she didn't want to be thrown back into the chaos of emotion that Holt Clavell seemed able to arouse in her. 'If you're sure you're not tired of me——?'

'*Tired* of you?' Pierre's hand went to his heart as he vowed, 'No man would be tired of such beauty! Is it not so, Edouard?'

Edouard agreed enthusiastically and the two girls exchanged looks of feminine scepticism, but Pierre's plan was accepted with pleasure.

Hours later the white coupé drew up outside the front door. Avis sighed sleepily; she shouldn't have drunk so much wine at dinner, she thought hazily.

'Thank you, Pierre, it's been a lovely day. I've never enjoyed myself so much.'

It was true, it had been a totally enjoyable day. Dinner at an intimate little restuarant set among the pine trees, with the four of them laughing their way through the courses of wonderful French food. Then dancing, and Pierre holding her close and whispering endearments into her hair. Just as Janice had predicted, Avis thought once or twice with a grin. This was what romance on the Riviera ought to be—light and happy, with no threat, no tearing at the emotions.

'I too,' he said in his quaint, formal way. 'A delightful day with delightful company.' His hand slid along the back of the seat and he drew her towards him. 'A kiss to complete the enjoyment of the day?'

He really was a sweetie. Avis put her arms round his neck and gave him back kiss for kiss and it was pleasant, but that was all—no wild tumult of the blood, no weakness in the knees, no drugging of the senses. Nothing that she had felt when Holt kissed her.

'Goodnight, Pierre, and thank you again.' She disengaged herself gently, and slipped out of the car and watched while it drove away. Then slowly she climbed the steps to the front door.

As she reached the top she went cold and her heart sank. The big, solid door confronted her, blank and firmly shut. How was she going to get in? Mrs Clavell would be in bed, Marie and Jacques would have gone home hours ago. That left Holt. She groaned inwardly. It was quite ridiculous, but she couldn't help feeling like a teenager who has stayed out late and is going to be scolded. She pushed the door, but it was unyielding. Oh well, she'd have to ring the bell and hope for the best.

She put up her hand to the bell-push and at the same moment the door swung open. Holt stood there, a tall, forbidding dark form silhouetted against the light.

'Oh—oh, thank you,' Avis stammered, walking past him into the hall. 'I'm sorry to disturb you.' He closed the door and locked it. Then he consulted his watch pointedly and moved across to the bottom of the staircase, blocking her way, looking her up and down superciliously.

'All dressed up like candy-floss,' he sneered. 'Very appropriate! I trust you've had a pleasant day.'

'Very pleasant, thank you. The Lemon Festival was great fun—very colourful.'

'Good.' He bit out the word. 'I suppose it didn't occur to you while you were having fun at——' he glanced again at his watch '—at two in the morning that you would be disturbing the household when you finally thought fit to come in.'

'I'm afraid it didn't. I'm so used to having my own key and coming and going as I please. I owe you an apology,' she added stiffly. 'I hope I haven't inconvenienced you too much.'

'Well, at least I had a front-row view of the tender parting scene,' he said nastily. 'I got the impression that it might be for my benefit. Playing hard to get, are you?'

'Rubbish!' Avis's cheeks were burning with anger and embarrassment. 'That implies that I want to be got—by you.'

'And of course you don't, do you?' Hands in pockets, he surveyed her insolently.

'No, I certainly don't.' She took a step towards the stairs but he didn't move.

'Whose idea was it—my mama's?' he said. 'She's

even deeper than I thought she was, bless her silly heart. She brought the dapper Pierre on the scene to provide a rival—to boost my male libido. And in case you're not familiar with the word, my child, it simply means lust.'

'Don't be so damned superior!' Avis flashed. 'Of course I know what libido means.'

He took a step nearer and his hand came out to burrow beneath the soft fall of hair and close on the nape of her neck. 'From personal experience?' he said softly.

'Let me go!' She tried to wriggle away, but his grasp only tightened. The touch of his fingers on her neck was making her inside tremble.

He looked down into her eyes, his lids lowered, hooded. 'I don't seem capable of taking my hands off you, do I?' His voice was husky. 'What are we going to do about it?'

She swallowed, searching desperately for words to cut him down to size, but nothing came. Neither did the strength to pull out of his grasp. His hand slid down to her waist, pressing her softness against his hard body. With his other hand he smoothed back her hair from her face.

'You have tempting hair,' he said.

'Tempting!' She laughed shakily because that sounded ridiculous.

Holt twisted a strand and wound it deliberately round her throat. 'Promise me you won't go out with that Pierre fellow again.'

She didn't know whether to take him seriously or not. 'Of course I won't promise, why should I?' she said lightly.

His eyes narrowed and the pressure on her throat increased. 'Promise me,' he repeated, and suddenly there was such violence in his voice that cold shivers ran all through her.

Her eyes stared up into his, wide and frightened. 'Go on, promise,' he ground out the words between his teeth.

'All right, I—I promise,' she muttered in a strangled voice, and felt the pressure on her throat relax.

She rubbed her neck, glaring up at him. 'That wasn't funny!'

'It wasn't meant to be funny.' He sounded almost surprised, as he said, quite slowly, 'You see, Mama's plan seems to have worked. Jealousy is something I haven't experienced up to now, but I could have murdered that fellow when I saw him kissing you.'

'Really?' she said coldly. 'Now, will you please let me go.' His arm was still holding her strongly and she bent backwards against it, ready to twist round and release herself.

'No, my sweet, I won't let you go,' he whispered against her ear. Then he began kissing her—her throat, her neck, her mouth; practised, arousing kisses that sent every memory of Pierre reeling from her mind. His fingers undid the buttons at the front of her low-necked dress deliberately, touching and stroking her skin gently, sending shudders through her whole body.

Avis felt her limbs go warm and pliant. Her arms went up round his neck as if pulled by cords, her fingers tangled in his hair, her mouth moved against his. Desire was wakening and clamouring inside her, new and overwhelming.

'I want you,' he muttered hungrily, 'and you want me, don't you, my darling? Let's go upstairs. Please, Avis!'

This was what she had expected—and dreaded. She shook her head desperately. 'No,' she said in a distraught voice. 'No!'

'Why not?' he murmured, and buried his mouth in the hollow of her shoulder.

She strove desperately for sanity. 'You wouldn't understand,' she muttered. He wouldn't understand that if she let him make love to her it would spoil any other man for her for years—perhaps for ever. She didn't know why she was so sure about this. Perhaps it was because she was in love with him.

He drew away a little, looking down into her face. 'Try me and see,' he said softly, teasingly. He was sure of her now, sure he could persuade her, and that awakened a vestige of self-respect in Avis. She *wasn't* going to let him take her like this, an easy target for his practised technique.

'No,' she said again loudly. 'I don't want it and I don't want you. I think you're arrogant and—and hateful! Now let me go.'

Holt dropped his arms immediately and his mouth twisted. 'Very well, we'll leave it for now.' His face looked very pale in the overhead lighting of the hall, but if she had wounded his pride he wasn't going to let her see it. 'Run along to bed then, little girl,' he sneered, 'and dream of the romantic French lad, if that's the kind of thing you prefer.'

It isn't, she shrieked silently. It's you I want, but I'm a coward. I'm afraid of being hurt, of being a plaything for a day or two and then being tossed aside, because that's what would happen. Oh God, she thought, I love him. That's why I daren't take the risk.

She turned away. 'Goodnight,' she muttered, and stumbled up the stairs and into her room. There was no need to lock her door—he wouldn't come after her. He wasn't the kind of man who would take rejection lightly. She sank down on to the dressing-table stool and stared at herself in the mirror, her face paper-white, her eyes enormous and aching with unshed tears. No use letting herself dissolve into sobs, that would come later perhaps. What she must do now was to get away. She was out of her depth with Holt Clavell—the only thing he would offer her would be a brief affair—even the insult of a one-night stand.

'No,' she said aloud, just as she had said it to him. She went on saying it while she threw off her clothes clumsily and slid into the soft bed. She was still murmuring it when she dropped into the sleep of utter exhaustion, more than an hour later.

It was after ten o'clock when Avis wakened next morning. She put a hand to her aching head and stared at the untouched breakfast tray on the table beside her bed. She dimly remembered Marie coming in with it, but she must have drifted off into an uneasy sleep again and now she felt terrible.

She drank a cup of tepid coffee, got up and showered, and felt slightly better. The new pink dress was in a crumpled heap on the floor and she folded it and packed it away in her travelling bag. Perhaps when it had been washed and ironed— perhaps some time in the future, next year maybe, she would be able to wear it again without remembering the painful end of what had, up to then, been a lovely romantic Riviera day.

She dressed in the plainest of her blouses and the skirt she had travelled in and went down to the kitchen to check with Marie that Mrs Clavell was awake. Then she climbed the stairs again and tapped at her hostess's door.

Mrs Clavell looked tired this morning. Her

cheeks were hollow and there were dark lines under her eyes.

'I haven't been sleeping very well lately,' she said, in reply to Avis's concerned enquiry. 'Dr Jago is prescribing some different tablets for me. Don't worry, my dear, I shall be quite all right tomorrow, and then perhaps I'll be able to go through those papers of mine. You're not in a terrible rush to get back to London, are you? Give Mr Hanworthy a ring and tell him I'd like you to stay on for a day or two longer.' The tired face suddenly looked eager. 'Go down and ring him now—there's a phone in the cloakroom downstairs—and then come back and tell me what he says.'

Avis ran down the wide staircase. This was playing straight into her hands, and she felt a twinge of guilt about deceiving Mrs Clavell. But on the other hand she felt almost convinced by now that she was herself being used by that lady, just as Holt had said. She supposed it might be a compliment that Mrs Clavell should consider her a suitable wife for her brilliant son. But on the other hand she didn't like being manipulated.

She went inside the cloakroom and closed the door firmly, after making sure that Holt wasn't lurking anywhere about, as he had been last night. She giggled feebly to herself as she looked up the international dialling code. She didn't really enjoy this M.I.6 cloak-and-dagger stuff. The thought occurred to her that Holt Clavell would make a perfect intelligence agent. He had the right kind of devious brain. Oh, stop thinking about the man, for goodness' sake, Avis. Just get away from him as quickly as possible.

She dialled and got through to Mr Hanworthy with amazing speed. It was somehow reassuring to hear the familiar voice asking her in his fatherly way how she was enjoying herself.

She gulped and said, 'Mr Hanworthy, this is going to sound rather ungrateful, but—but I want to come back to London straight away. I'll explain when I see you.' (She could make up some explanation on the plane.) 'Would you mind if I told Mrs Clavell that you needed me back at the earliest possible moment?'

'Would I mind? No, of course, not, Avis. I shall be extremely glad to have you back. So you can get your skates on, my girl.'

Avis smiled. Dear Mr Hanworthy! It would be nice to get back to his pleasant, undemanding company.

When she had said goodbye to him she rang the airport at Nice and found that there was a cancelled flight she could have that afternoon. Then she went back to Mrs Clavell's room.

'To leave today?' echoed that lady in a dismayed voice. 'But you can't go so soon!'

'I'm terribly sorry,' Avis said regretfully, feeling a fraud. 'It seems very ungrateful when you've been so kind to me, but Mr Hanworthy needs me urgently in London and—well, he's my boss and I can't very well refuse.'

'No, my dear, I see that, but—what time will you have to leave?'

Avis glanced at her watch. 'In less than an hour, I suppose, to catch my flight. I could get a taxi to the airport, perhaps——'

'Oh no, certainly not. Jacques will drive you. What a pity Holt isn't here, he could have driven you to Nice himself. Oh dear—then you may not see Holt again before you go. He went out early and I'm not sure when he'll be back.' Mrs Clavell's fingers plucked nervously at the satin quilt on her bed. She looked really upset. 'I'd hoped—but there, it was a forlorn hope, I see that now.'

So Holt was right—his mother *had* been using her as bait in her plot to get Holt married! She should have been angry, but as she looked at the frail woman propped up in the big bed she couldn't feel anything but pity. Mrs Clavell seemed so alone, and—for all her wealth and her two lovely houses—somehow pathetic.

It seemed fitting that the weather had changed by the time Avis was ready to leave. There was no sunshine today and a cold drizzle of rain was falling as she walked down the steps to where Jacques was waiting with the car. Taking leave of her hostess had been rather a strain. Mrs Clavell had held out her arms to Avis and kissed her, and the tears had gathered in her eyes.

'It's been so lovely to have someone young and pretty with me,' she sighed. 'I shall miss you, Avis. Please do come and see us when I get back to England in the summer. Promise you will.'

'I'd love to,' said Avis, and knew that she would never go. Never, so long as there was the slightest risk of encountering Holt again. There were only two ways of meeting danger—flight or fight. She could never fight him again, she knew that. She had almost given way under the strain last night; she wouldn't have the strength to resist if she found herself in his arms again. If it had merely been that she fancied him, then everything might have been different, but it was so much more than that. In two days Avis had fallen deeply and irrevocably in love.

'Ready, *mademoiselle*?' Jacques opened the car door and Avis was about to climb in when Holt's car pulled round the corner of the drive and stopped with a spurt of gravel. Holt got out and walked across to Avis.

'Where are you off to?' he demanded abruptly.

'I'm leaving,' said Avis, not meeting his eyes. 'Recalled to duty,' she added lightly.

Out of the corner of her eye she saw someone else approaching and realised that Hélène Jago had arrived with Holt and was sauntering up to them to stand beside him. She wore black today with an ornate silver chain round her neck and she looked every inch the sophisticated career woman, her sleek head held at a self-assured angle, her thin lips curved disdainfully. Avis could well see why Mrs Clavell found her doctor lacking in human warmth.

She acknowledged Avis with a casual nod, and laid a hand on Holt's arm, speaking rapidly to him in French, which Avis couldn't understand. He replied, and after a moment's hesitation the woman turned and walked up the steps towards the house.

Holt turned back to Avis. 'What did you mean—you're leaving?' His face was a hard mask, and there was a note in his voice that made her stomach quiver with fear.

'Just that,' she said, swallowing. 'Mr Hanworthy needs me back in London immediately and I've been fortunate in getting a flight on this afternoon's plane. Jacques is driving me to the airport.'

'I see,' he said tightly. 'And what has my mother to say about that? I understood that she was relying on you to be her courier—to take her papers back to London when she'd finished with them.'

'I've explained to Mrs Clavell,' Avis told him. His closeness was beginning to have its usual effect on her breathing, tightening her throat and making her voice husky. 'She quite understands.'

He stared at her for a long moment in silence. Then he said abruptly, 'Are you telling the truth?'

Her eyes widened. 'What on earth do you mean?'

'I mean,' he said deliberately, 'are you running away?'

She shook her head, managing a bewildered smile. 'I haven't the least idea what you're talking about.'

Holt put out a hand and grasped hers, so tightly that it seemed as if her bones would crumble. 'I mean—are you running away from me? Or from yourself?' His eyes burned with suppressed anger. 'You know damned well that we started something. I didn't think you were a quitter, Avis.'

She couldn't any longer pretend not to understand. She shrugged. 'Then I'm afraid you'll have to put up with it. Now, will you please release my hand? Goodbye, Mr Clavell, it's been quite an experience, meeting you. Perhaps I may see you in court one of these days. I'm sure you'll be terrific.' As Jacques leaned over and put his head out of the window at the passenger side she called, 'All right, Jacques, I'm coming now.'

Holt seemed, for once, to be struck dumb, and his face was set and angry. She had got under his arrogant guard finally. She climbed into the car, giving Jacques a brilliant smile. 'It's so good of you to drive me, Jacques, and I'm quite ready now.'

The big car hummed into life and moved forward, Avis sitting straight beside the driver. She didn't look back to see if Holt had joined Hélène Jago.

It didn't matter to her any longer, she assured herself. If she had made a tiny dent in his self-assurance, no doubt that smooth lady would soon straighten it out. She had won the battle over herself. She had done what she thought was best. She should be feeling triumphant. Instead, Holt's words were eating into her brain—'Are you running away from me? Or from yourself? I didn't think you were a quitter, Avis.'

Yes, she should be feeling triumphant. Instead she had an appalling feeling that she had done something mean and despicable. It wasn't fair of him, she told herself defiantly, to make her feel like that. He had made all the running and she had resisted. But she hadn't resisted very convincingly. She remembered how she had pressed herself against him, kissing him back with an abandonment that made her blood run hot just to remember.

She sat staring through the windscreen at the road ahead. Yesterday it had been sunny and full of people, enjoying themselves. Today, in the drizzling rain, everything was grey and depressing.

'It is a pity you leave us so soon, *mademoiselle*,' Jacques told her in his careful English. 'You should have stayed longer.'

Tears gathered thickly in Avis's eyes. 'Perhaps I should, Jacques,' she said.

CHAPTER FIVE

THE drizzle in Menton had become a steady downpour by the time Avis reached London. It was the end of the rush-hour, and the journey from Heathrow by coach and tube was a nightmare. When she finally reached the flat she climbed the stairs to the first floor and almost fell inside, dropping her bag in the hall.

Janice's surprised face appeared round the kitchen door. 'Avis!' she screamed. 'What are you doing here? You're supposed to be lapping up the sunshine on the Riviera!' She came across the hall as Avis leaned exhaustedly against the front door. 'Golly, you look all in, chum, and you're *dripping* wet! Here, let me peel your mac off.'

'I had to walk from the station, there wasn't a taxi.' Avis staggered into the kitchen and slumped into a chair, pulling off her sandals. 'Is that coffee I smell?'

'Just made.' Janice filled a beaker and passed it to Avis, who cradled it in her cold hands. Was it possible that only yesterday she had walked by the sea in a cotton dress with the sun warm on her hair? She shivered.

'So what happened?' Janice looked at her curiously, and when Avis didn't seem inclined to answer she fell back on her usual topic of interest. 'Didn't the romance of the Riviera come up to scratch, then?' Her eyes were teasing under her thick, straight fringe. 'No tall, dark, handsome stranger fold you in his arms, eh?'

Avis took a sip of coffee and tried to think of

something to say to match Janice's lighthearted banter. She shook her head mutely.

Janice giggled. 'Bad luck, pal, I always thought the sunny Mediterranean couldn't be as terrific as it's cracked up to be, and I've heard that the men around there have some chauvinist-piggy ways with girls.'

'Oh, but——' Avis began. Then suddenly everything was too much and the tears that she had been holding back all the way on the plane gushed up and spilled over and she began to sob helplessly. The holiday that had promised so much had turned out terribly, desperately wrong. It wasn't her scene, she should never have gone.

Janice put down her coffee mug and jumped up, hugging her tightly. 'What have I said, love? Me and my big mouth!'

Avis didn't often cry and she hated losing control of herself. 'I'm sorry—so sorry—stupid of me,' she hiccuped between sobs.

At last the tears stopped. She blew her nose and grinned at Janice wryly. Janice grinned back. 'That did you good, I guess. Better to get it out of your system. A man, was it?' she added in her practical way. 'It usually is.' She sat down again and picked up her mug of coffee.

'Yes,' Avis croaked. She had never indulged in cosy girl-to-girl chats about boy-friends with Janice—or with anyone else, but now the temptation to unburden herself was too strong. 'You see, I—I had to get away.'

'Hm,' Janice nodded knowingly. 'Like that, was it?'

Avis looked up quickly. 'Like what?'

'Some of 'em can be right bastards,' said Janice, shrugging, with a tinge of bitterness in her voice. 'Cruel. I don't go for that myself.'

'Oh no, he wasn't——' Avis said quickly. 'Not what you mean.' Yet the memory suddenly came to her of the way Holt had twisted her hair round her neck, of the savage note in his voice that had frightened her. 'It was just that he—he didn't——'

Janice stared at her, blue eyes wide. 'You're not telling me that he didn't fall for you,' she said. 'That I won't believe. You're smashing, Avis. Any man looking at you would want you.'

'Oh, he wanted me all right.' Avis's lips thinned and she picked up her coffee beaker again.

'Well then——?'

It was all so simple to Janice, Avis thought wearily, and wished it could be to her. She pursed her lips, shaking her head. 'Just going to bed with him would have been——' she groped for the right word and couldn't find it '—no use,' she finished, shrugging.

Janice stared at her for a long time, then shook her head. 'I don't get it,' she said. 'You're too romantic for this tough world, chum.' She looked keenly at Avis. 'You're not a virgin, are you?' She saw the answer in her friend's face. 'Well, blow me down, I didn't think there were any left.'

'Then you were wrong,' Avis said shortly.

Janice looked contrite. 'Don't mind me, love, my tongue's always tripping me up, as my grandma used to say. The words slip out without my thinking. I didn't mean to pry, and anyway it's your own business.'

'It doesn't matter,' said Avis. 'Forget it. That's what I'm going to do—forget the whole wretched business.'

There was an awkward silence, then Avis stood up. 'I'll go and get out of these clothes. Is the shower working yet?'

Janice nodded eagerly, obviously anxious to

atone for her tactlessness. 'I chivvied the electric people until they actually sent a man round yesterday. It's O.K. now.' She glanced doubtfully at Avis. 'There's some chicken-and-ham pie in the fridge. Jane's gone to Ken's for the evening and I've got a date. A new man, he's rather super.' She giggled. 'He works in Sainsbury's, in the delicatessen department—that's where the pie came from. We're eating very well just at present!' She glanced doubtfully at Avis. 'You'll be O.K., Ave?'

Avis turned to the bedroom door. 'I'll be fine,' she said. 'Thanks for the coffee, Jan. Have a good time.' She summoned a smile.

In the days that followed Avis had to make more and more of an effort to smile. She had told herself she would get over Holt quite quickly when she got back into routine again. After all, nothing much had happened between them. He had kissed her a couple of times; he had wanted to spend a night with her. Nothing earth-shaking about that. Instead, the nagging feeling of emptiness inside got worse, and time didn't seem to have anything to do with it. She dragged herself through the days like a zombie, doing her job automatically, aware that Mr Hanworthy gave her some odd looks but had the tact not to ask questions.

It was worse at the flat. Jane's wedding was less than a week away and even the quiet, self-contained Jane was excited and starry-eyed. The whole flat was a continual reminder of married bliss to come. China and glass and cutlery and kitchen appliances were piled on every horizontal space in the living room. Jane had given her friends lists of the presents she would appreciate, all of which were useful and none of which were frivolous. Sensible Jane!

Avis went out and bought the most expensive steam iron she could find and tied the parcel up with looped bows of white ribbon, the way the vendeuse had tied her dress-boxes in Menton. Just doing that brought the whole of those days' happenings back so vividly that she had to shut herself in the loo so that nobody would see or hear her sobs.

You're really being very wet, she scolded herself. She'd never had much time for girls who indulged in nervous breakdowns when an affair folded up on them. She didn't think she was heading for a nervous breakdown and there hadn't been any affair. Perhaps that was the trouble, she brooded miserably. Perhaps if I'd gone to bed with him when he wanted me to that night, I'd have got him out of my system. Perhaps I would, by now, have got over this awful sick yearning to see him, to hear his voice. Perhaps.

Four days after she got back a bulky parcel arrived at the office, addressed to Mr Hanworthy and marked 'Personal'. The postmark was Menton. Avis's heart plummeted as she took it in to him and she knew she had been secretly hoping that Holt would himself bring his mother's papers in when he returned to England.

She put the parcel down on Mr Hanworthy's desk. 'These will be Mrs Clavell's papers,' she said. She kept her voice studiedly noncommittal.

He looked up. 'The papers you were supposed to stay to bring back?' he asked mildly. She had heard him use that tone to clients when he wanted to get some information out of them which they weren't volunteering.

'Yes,' she replied, giving nothing away.

He slanted a look at her under his bushy grey

eyebrows. 'Yes, open it. We may as well see if she's changed her will.'

Avis picked up the pocket knife that Mr Hanworthy kept on the desk-tidy and began to prise out the staples. Whoever had packed the parcel had made a good job of it. Had Holt done it? she wondered. Was he still there with his mother—and with Dr Hélène Jago? Jealousy stirred painfully in her stomach. The penknife slipped on a staple, and blood spurted from her thumb. She sucked it and waved away Mr Hanworthy's concern. 'It's nothing—look, it's stopped bleeding now.'

'One can't be too careful.' Mr Hanworthy opened a desk drawer and took out a small first-aid outfit. 'Here, let me put one of these tiddly little bandages on.'

'Oh really, it's nothing,' Avis demurred as Mr Hanworthy carefully cleaned the blood away with antiseptic and applied a bandage.

'Never take a cut lightly,' her chief lectured, and quoted solemnly, ' "He jests at scars who never felt a wound." Shakespeare. *Romeo and Juliet*, if I'm correct—that wonderful and most unhappy romance!' He gave the bandage a little pat and eyed her quizzically. 'I'm wondering if an unhappy romance has been your experience in France and that was why you had to return early? Tell me to mind my own business if you like, my dear.'

She smiled crookedly at him. He was such a dear, and so perceptive.

'How clever of you to guess,' she said.

'I have daughters of my own,' Mr Hanworthy reminded her. 'I know how these things go.' He cleared his throat. 'Dare I hope for a satisfactory outcome?'

Avis shook her head. 'Not a chance.' She looked

up quickly into the kind, elderly face. 'Have I been a misery since I came back? I'm so sorry—I hope my work hasn't suffered.'

'Your work, as always, has been faultless, Avis,' Mr Hanworthy assured her. He was unpacking the parcel as he spoke and now he took a letter from the top. 'Ah—from Mrs Clavell's son, Holt. He was down there with her, was he? How did you get on with him?'

Avis's eyes went to the firm black writing on the sheet of notepaper and she felt the colour drain from her cheeks. 'He was—he was——' she began. What could she say? Her throat dried and she couldn't speak.

Mr Hanworthy raised his eyes from the sheet of paper and studied her face thoughtfully. 'Ah,' he said again, and she knew that he guessed. After that he didn't speak of the matter again, for which Avis was grateful.

Two days later, Avis placed a batch of letters for signing on Mr Hanworthy's desk. 'I know we're very busy and I hesitate to ask,' she said, 'but could I possibly take a few hours off on Thursday? One of my flatmates is getting married.'

Mr Hanworthy agreed immediately, but Avis thought she saw a faintly worried look cross his face. They were indeed very busy—engaged in some highly confidential work, which involved drawing up lengthy and complicated contracts, and she knew that Mr Hanworthy wouldn't care to entrust any of the typing to one of the other girls in the office. 'The ceremony is early—ten o'clock,' she went on quickly, '—so it should all be over by midday. I'll come straight back and stay late if necessary.'

'My dear girl, you can't come back to do dreary

office work after the celebrations! You'll want to stay on and enjoy yourself.'

Her eyes met his and her smile was very wry. 'I won't, you know,' she said quietly, and she saw that he took the point. 'I'll be quite glad to get away.'

Jane's wedding was a very small quiet affair at the local Congregational Church—just Kenneth's parents and Jane's uncle (her only relative) who had travelled down from Leeds for the occasion. Two of Kenneth's friends, two girls from Jane's office, and Avis and Janice, and that completed the party. Jane had decided that they would hold the reception at the flat. 'Stupid to spend all that money on a hotel,' she had said, and she had been up half the night finishing the icing on the cake.

Jane had planned everything down to the last detail, as Kenneth was studying hard for his exams, so—as with everything Jane planned—it all went like clockwork. Jane's homemade dress looked elegant and Janice had set her hair the night before and helped with her make-up, and she really did look very attractive and very happy and pleased with life as she gazed up at her new husband, in his new navy-blue pin-striped suit, making his speech.

Avis drank the toast in sparkling white wine, and felt that they would have a good marriage. They were two of a pair, two rather serious young people to whom life was real, life was earnest. They might be a little dull, but if they never reached the heights, at least they wouldn't know that they were missing anything.

As soon as the couple left for their honeymoon in Devon, Avis slipped away back to the office. For some reason that she didn't want to examine the wedding had left her vaguely depressed and she was glad to get back to her typewriter.

Mr Hanworthy was quite obviously glad to see her back, although he tried not to make it too obvious. 'Sorry you had to leave the festivities,' he said. 'It's good of you to come back, my dear, and you're looking very attractive, if an old man may be permitted a compliment.'

'Thank you.' Avis smiled at him affectionately. He really was a cherub—like one of Dickens's benevolent old gentlemen who put everything right in the end. It was a pity, she thought wryly, that he couldn't do that for her.

At the tea-break the other girls admired her outfit too. Avis was wearing the pink and cream dress she had bought in Menton. She had stuffed it in her bag when she left, but after pressing it had come out fresh again, and she couldn't afford another new dress for the wedding anyway. After this occasion, she promised herself, it would be hidden away in the back of her wardrobe. She could do without reminders of those few days when her emotions had been working at fever pitch.

The contract had to be completed before she left this evening and she worked steadily all through the afternoon, keeping her mind resolutely on the job. At half past five Mr Hanworthy put his head round the door of the small office. 'How's it going, Avis?'

'About another three-quarters of an hour should see it through,' she said, pushing back her hair from her damp forehead. The rather antiquated central heating was apt to get oppressive in the late afternoon.

He nodded. 'I'll just slip round and see Johnson myself and tell him the contracts should be with him tomorrow. Shan't be long.' The door closed behind him.

Everyone else had gone home; there wasn't a sound in the office. Avis wondered if she should bolt the big front door, but Mr Hanworthy had said he wouldn't be long, so she sat where she was and for a moment or two rested her elbows on her desk and buried her face in her hands, not thinking of anything in particular, just wishing this grey nothingness that surrounded her since she got back from Menton would go away. She really must make an effort to get back to normal.

Normal meant Robert. She wondered if he was still angry with her. Perhaps she would phone him and find out. He would have left the bank by now, but she might catch him at home. Her hand went out to the phone on her desk and stopped. If he knew she had come back early he would probably say, 'I told you so,' and she didn't think she could bear that. She sighed, pulled the typewriter closer, and went on with her work.

The minutes dragged by; the small office got hotter and the typed characters on the thick, legal paper began to dance crazily before Avis's tired eyes. She rubbed a place on her temple that was beginning to ache and carried on.

Ten minutes or so later she heard the footsteps in the passage. Mr Hanworthy's office door opened and then the communicating door to her own office opened.

'Nearly finished,' she called cheerfully without stopping typing. 'Nearly through now. Give me another five minutes.'

'I'll give you all the time in the world, Avis,' said Holt Clavell's deep voice.

Her hands dropped nervelessly into her lap. Shock held her motionless, everything inside her clenched rigid. Then she spun the typing chair.

'What are you doing here?' It was unbelievable

that her voice should sound ordinary, when her heart was thudding in her throat. 'Mr Hanworthy's out at the moment.'

'I haven't come to see Mr Hanworthy,' he said. 'I've come to see you.' He strolled across and stood beside her desk, resting one hand on it. She stared down at the long, sinewy fingers with their immaculately-tended nails and saw with amazement that his hand was not quite steady. Her eyes lifted to his face, wide with bewilderment.

'When did you get back?' she said stupidly.

He glanced at his watch. 'About an hour ago, to be exact.'

Avis met his eyes as he watched her face under lowered lids and for a long, long moment they stared at each other in silence. Avis felt that she was going to faint. The air of the office had been too warm before, but now there seemed to be no air to breathe at all. She put a hand to her throat.

'Your mother's documents arrived safely a day or two ago.'

'Oh, good,' he said without interest, and was silent again.

Outside, traffic rumbled past in the main road. Inside the office there was no sound except for the steady tick of the clock above the door. Avis's nerves felt as if they were slowly splintering, like a car windscreen after a violent collision. If he didn't speak she was going to scream.

'Why are you here? What do you want with me?' she asked, with a tremendous effort.

The hand on her desk relaxed and dropped to his side. 'I want you to come out to dinner with me,' he said, and added, with a faint twist of his long mouth, 'for a start.'

For the second time in two minutes surprise took her breath away.

'Will you?' he said. 'And don't say you're not dressed for an evening out, because I can see you are. And very nice too.' His eyes ran slowly over the cream and pink outfit.

'Candy-floss?' she murmured, and wished she hadn't, as she saw from the look in his eyes that he was remembering exactly the occasion when he had said that, just as she was herself. Remembering, too, what had come afterwards.

He smiled faintly. 'I do not admit that as evidence for the prosecution,' he said. He put a hand lightly on her shoulder and she felt a shudder pass through her. 'Come on, Avis, say you will.'

'I—I——' she croaked, then mumbled inelegantly. 'All right, but you'll have to wait until I've finished.'

Avis didn't realise that Mr Hanworthy had come in until she heard a discreet cough from his office next door. She jumped to her feet quickly. 'Mr Hanworthy, this is Mr Clavell—Mr Holt Clavell. I don't know if you've met him.'

The elderly solicitor held out a hand. 'Happy to make your acquaintance, Mr Clavell. Your reputation in the law has preceded you, I may say.' He beamed at the younger man and then at Avis. 'I—er—take it that your visit is not concerned with legal matters?'

Holt smiled charmingly. 'With your permission, sir, I came to invite your secretary to come out to dinner with me. I'm delighted to say that she has accepted.'

'Not until I've finished typing the contract,' Avis snapped, glaring at Holt angrily. What was he up to? What did he want of her? She didn't trust him an inch, and why she had so weakly agreed to go to dinner with him she couldn't imagine. And yet part of her, somewhere deep inside, was in a turmoil.

Mr Hanworthy nodded. 'I have that jewel without price,' he said solemnly, 'a secretary with integrity. Come, Mr Clavell, we'll go into my office and perhaps you'll join me in a sherry, while Avis is completing her work.'

Completing the work was a nightmare. One mistake and the whole page would have to be re-typed. Somehow Avis managed to slow down, concentrate, and produce a perfect final page. She sat back in her chair, closing her eyes, breathing jerkily as she heard the voices of the two men in the next office, Mr Hanworthy's genial and humorous, evidently recounting a story; Holt's deep and amused, putting in a word here and there. Then he laughed. I've never heard him laugh like that—really laugh, Avis thought with surprise. With her, and even with his mother, he had always been ironic, enigmatic. But that laugh seemed to make him more approachable. more human.

She took the final page of the contract into Mr Hanworthy's office and laid it on the desk in front of him, not looking at Holt, but flutteringly aware of him sitting at ease in the visitor's chair.

'Good girl—splendid!' Mr Hanworthy beamed. 'Thank you for putting yourself out about it, Avis.' He looked across to Holt. 'This excellent young lady actually left a wedding celebration to come back to the office and finish this urgent bit of work. How's that for dedication?'

'Ah,' drawled Holt, 'but I already appreciate her value, Mr Hanworthy. A jewel without price, didn't you say?'

Avis could usually take teasing as well as the next girl, but now she flushed with annoyance and embarrassment. She turned on her heel and went out of the office. She tidied her desk, taking her time over it, then went into the girls' room, rinsed her face and put on fresh make-up, smoothing it carefully over her hot cheeks. Inside she was a seething cauldron of emotions, but at least she could present a calm exterior.

The pink and cream blouse with the frilly collar was as fresh and crisp as it had been when she put it on this morning. She took her short jacket out of her locker and shrugged into it, then looked at her reflection in the mirror. It was amazing—she looked cool and sleek and poised. And that's how I'm going to stay, so help me, she vowed. However difficult it is I won't let him see how he's got under my skin. Picking up her handbag, she marched out of the cloakroom.

Holt had a taxi waiting outside the office and he handed Avis in and followed. Avis sat in the corner of the seat—not far enough to look as if she was burrowing in like a frightened animal, but not near enough for Holt to touch her. He made no attempt to touch her, however. He sat back in his own corner as the taxi headed towards Town, with a small smile on his mouth and a glint in his grey-green eyes, looking at her as if he found this whole situation vastly amusing.

Avis had to break the silence. 'How is Mrs Clavell?' she enquired.

'Mama is very well,' he said, 'although she doesn't admit it. I got Dr Jago to look her over and it was a clean bill of health.'

'I'm very glad,' said Avis. Perhaps she had just been imagining that Mrs Clavell had looked really unwell just before she left.

'I may say,' Holt went on, and a faintest of twinkles lit his eyes, 'that she cheered up considerably when I told her I was going to see you when I got back to London.'

She glanced at him and then away again, quickly. 'I do wish you wouldn't go on about this,' she said. 'I'm sure you're making all this up about your mother trying to get you married off. Mothers don't behave like that these days.'

He chuckled. 'Mine does,' he said. 'You've no idea. Still, it has given me an opportunity to see you again, if only to make up for the way I misjudged you at first. I was going to ask you to have dinner with me at Gaston's, only you ran away from me.'

'I ran away from *you*?' she cried indignantly. 'I never did!' And forgive me for that whopping great lie.

'No? Well, let it pass. Look, let's call a truce and have a pleasant evening together. Shall we?'

She looked at him across the width of the jolting taxi and he was smiling—little crinkles fanning out beside his eyes. She hadn't believed he could smile like that, as if he really meant it. He looked quite different—younger, not angry, or arrogant, or sarcastic. He looked devastatingly handsome too, his dark hair brushed firmly away from his face, his thick-lashed eyelids lowered over glinting grey eyes. Her look traced the shape of his mouth and she felt a strong stirring inside.

Holt reached out and covered her hand with his and she flinched as if he had touched a raw nerve. 'Don't be afraid of me, Avis,' he said softly. 'I wouldn't harm you—ever.'

She blinked, amazed. She couldn't believe that there was tenderness in his voice. What had happened to make such a difference in him? It couldn't merely be that at last he believed her when she said she wasn't plotting with his mother.

But whatever the reason, it was a wonderful change. Suddenly she felt light as air; all the gloom of the past days had lifted away, like the sun breaking through a thick grey mist. 'Well, that's a nice change,' she laughed, and for the first time she felt easy with him, as if she could say anything to him. 'It wasn't so long ago that you threatened to strangle me, I seem to remember!'

'Don't hold that against me, I was out of my mind. I'd been picturing what was going on between you and that Pierre fellow for hours. Mama's little ploy certainly worked.'

'You still think she arranged it all?'

'I'm certain she did. His mother is a bridge partner of hers. I bet they cooked it up together,' he said darkly.

'I liked Pierre, he's a very nice boy,' Avis said demurely. 'He gave me a lovely day at the Festival. It was absolutely fascinating, how they could make all those super set-pieces from lemons and oranges—the decorations in the gardens were out of this world, and the girls were beautiful in their pretty Provençal costumes——'

She chattered on nervously, aware that Holt had moved towards her. His arm went along the top of the seat and every fibre of her body quivered in response. She kept her head turned away, staring out of the taxi window at the lights of the thick traffic, swirling in the dusk, her hands clenched.

'Avis?' Her name was a husky whisper.

Like someone in a dream she turned her head and saw the glint of his eyes fixed on her in the shadowy dimness inside the taxi. His other arm came out and gathered her against him, his mouth claiming hers in a kiss that went on and on, exciting her more with every moment until she thought she would faint.

At last he drew away a little, his eyes searching her face. 'God, I needed that,' he groaned. 'Cool spring water to a man dying of thirst!'

He laughed a little at that, he wasn't taking the kiss too seriously. He was a passionate man, easily aroused, she guessed. Proximity would always be a temptation he would find it hard to resist. She mustn't let herself read more into his actions than he intended. This invitation meant nothing momentous. He had looked her up because he felt a trifle guilty about her, that was all.

The taxi was bowling along the Edgware Road now, moving briskly against the main stream of traffic leaving town. Holt moved back to his corner again. 'It's safer here,' he said with a smile in his voice.

Avis touched the warm leather of the seat beside her where he had sat, storing up every little detail of this magic moment: the rumbling of the traffic, the curious enclosed intimacy of the taxi, the slightly fusty smell that all taxis seem to have, the worn springing of the seat, the dark bulk of the driver behind his glass partition. And Holt here with her—the man who she wanted beside her more than any other man in the whole world. It seemed like a miracle.

'Where would you like to go for dinner?' he asked. 'Do you fancy the bright lights or something more cosy?'

'I leave it to you,' said Avis. She felt incapable of making up her mind about anything just at present.

'That's what I like to hear.' He tapped on the glass partition and said something to the driver, and a few minutes later the taxi pulled up in a dark little side street and Holt got out and held out his hand to her.

After that the evening got more and more dreamlike. The small restaurant was like a cavern, hushed and dimly-lit, with ankle-deep carpets and the scent of freesias filling the room. They sat at a table in an alcove and Holt ordered for them both and the food tasted heavenly, though Avis couldn't have said what she was eating. The wine bubbled in her glass and she seemed to be bubbling too with sheer joy. Somewhere at the back of her mind a tiny voice warned, 'Make the most of it, Avis, this is a one-off thing,' but she ignored it.

Holt did all the talking, which was fine, because all she needed to do was to smile at him and murmur words that sounded as if they made sense. He told her amusing stories about his work in the courts and the cases he had had recently. He talked a bit about the family home in the Cotswolds that his mother loved so dearly. While he talked she could look her fill at him across the table, revelling in the way the crinkles came and went beside his eyes, and the quirk of his mouth, and the turn of his dark head. Oh lord, she thought, I've fallen fathoms deep in love with him, but there's nothing I can do about it.

'It's all been about me,' he said at last, as he poured more wine into her glass. 'Tell me about you.'

'Me?' She was startled out of a dream. 'I'm not a very interesting subject. What do you want to know?'

'Everything,' he said simply, and smiled into her eyes.

'Oh!' She felt the colour run into her cheeks and was thankful for the dimness of the light. 'Well, let's see. Twenty years old, brown eyes, light brown hair, five feet three, small mole on left shoulder.'

'That,' he said with a grin, 'I must see. Go on. Place of residence?'

'Flat in Chingford, shared with two other girls— no, only one now. The other one got married this morning. She had the reception in the flat. I dread to think what kind of a mess it's in now!' When he took her home that would provide an excuse for not inviting him to come in, which she certainly didn't intend to do.

'Job?' he said. 'We know that, don't we?'

'Yes, secretary to Mr Hanworthy, solicitor, who's a poppet.'

'Parents?'

There was a pause and when she spoke her tone had changed. 'My father died when I was a baby. He was in the R.A.F. and he was killed in an accident. My mother brought me up alone. It must have been a struggle for her because she was only eighteen when my father died. She's rather special—the old thing about being more like sisters than mother and daughter seems true with us.'

'And where is she now?'

Avis's eyes clouded. 'In Australia. She married again a year ago—she could have married lots of times, I'm sure of that, but I don't think anyone could take my father's place. Until Rick came along. Then she fell in love again and that was that. They wanted me to go out to Australia with them. It was quite a temptation, but I finally decided to stay and learn to stand on my own two feet, as the saying goes.'

'I'm glad you did,' said Holt quietly. 'You won't go, will you?'

His eyes held hers and there was an expression in them that set her inside churning.

'I might, some day,' she said, with a brave attempt at lightness.

Coffee and liqueurs were finished and the waiter had cleared the table. Holt called for the bill, saying, 'We'll move on, shall we?'

Move on—where to? Avis wondered feverishly as she dabbed her flushed cheeks with cool lotion-pads in the ladies' powder room. If he suggested a night club she would refuse politely, she decided. It had been a perfect evening, to prolong it might spoil the magic.

Outside the restaurant London had settled into its evening phase. In Piccadilly Circus the neon lights flashed garishly, trying to outshine a full moon that sailed above them in a black sky, and failing miserably. Youths and girls wandered along, entwined, or lingered in doorways. Cars braked at the crossings, panted impatiently at red lights, and swooped away again.

Holt put an arm round Avis's shoulders. 'You're cold,' he said, as she shivered. 'That pretty outfit was bought for warmer climes, wasn't it?' He hailed a passing taxi and it pulled up. Avis thought hazily that he was the kind of man for whom taxis always stop.

He spoke to the driver and got in beside her. 'I have a small bachelor pad in Chelsea,' he told her. 'I told him to go there. I'm sure you won't want to attack your own post-wedding-reception chaos at this time of the evening. I'll take you back just in time to fall into bed and forget the tidying up until the morning. How about that?'

It sounded so practical and ordinary, it would seem stupid to refuse. Avis closed her mind to what might be assumed by a man when a girl agrees to go to his flat at night.

On the short drive to Chelsea she lay back in a

warm haze, knowing quite well that she had drunk
far too much wine at dinner and with a growing
feeling of recklessness stealing over her, softening
all her senses. Janice would be proud of me, she
thought.

Holt's 'pad' was on the first floor of an old
house in a side street off the Chelsea Embankment.
He switched on a subdued light and drew the
heavy blue velvet curtains over the long windows
that led out on to an iron balcony. 'It's pleasant
here,' he said. 'Fairly quiet, and on a clear day, if
you twist your neck, you can see the river.' He
chuckled, pulling off his jacket and tossing it over
a chair, as he switched on the electric fire.

'What shall we drink?' He turned to a side table
at the other end of the long, elegant living room.

Avis sank into a deep chair and was swallowed up
by velvet cushions. 'Is it possible to make tea?' She
laughed nervously. 'I've got the kind of thirst that
only tea can quench.' Making tea would take a little
time. Would put off the moment when— when——

'Of course it's possible,' he said promptly. 'I
have a kitchen the size of a birdcage, but making
tea is one of its accomplishments. I'm partial to tea
myself, so that's one thing we agree about. No
doubt,' he added, coming back across the room to
her, 'we shall discover others in due course.' He
held out a hand and pulled her out of the chair.
'Come and tell me which brand you fancy.'

The kitchen was tiny but extravagantly
equipped. Holt put on a kettle to boil, while Avis
exclaimed over all the built-in modern gadgets.
'It's fascinating,' she said. 'You've got everything
here to cook with.' She touched the microwave
oven. 'I've always wanted one of these. They're so
useful when you have to get a meal at short notice,
or if guests drop in or something.' She prattled

away nervously while Holt leaned against the sink and never took his eyes from her face.

At last she could think of nothing more to say and fell into an uneasy silence. The kettle boiled and Holt indicated a row of tea canisters on a shelf. 'Just tea, please,' Avis murmured. 'Nothing fancy.'

She went back into the living room, leaving him to carry the tray. She walked over to the window and pulled back the velvet curtains, looking down at the street below, seeing nothing. She was rigid with nerves. Why had she come here with him? Oh, why? It wasn't her scene, she must have been mad. She would drink one cup of tea and then ask him to take her home. Insist on it.

She turned as he came into the room, carrying the tray. He put it down on a low table by the glowing electric fire. They stood looking at each other across the width of the room. He seemed to have nothing to say either. For what seemed an eternity their looks locked and held and she couldn't take her eyes off him, standing tall and elegant in his immaculately-cut black trousers and white silk shirt. A trembling started inside her, rising from her legs up her body until she felt she would fall over, and clutched at the back of a chair.

In the subdued lighting his eyes were dark mysterious lakes under their hooded lids; she could hear his breathing, shallow and uneven. Very slowly he held out his arms to her. 'Avis,' he muttered huskily. 'Come here to me.'

Through her confusion one thing stood out. He wasn't going to touch her or try to arouse her. She must make the decision herself. And suddenly there was no decision to make. She loved him.

'Avis?' he said again.

She stumbled across the room into his arms.

CHAPTER SIX

At first he held her tightly against him as if he would never let her go. His cheek rubbed against her hair as he murmured soft endearments. 'Little Avis—sweetheart, I thought I'd lost you—please tell me you don't hate me, that we can start afresh——'

Tears gathered thickly in her eyes because what was happening was so incredible and so wonderful. Surely she would wake up in a moment and find none of it was true. She couldn't speak, but she reached up and turned his head until their mouths were touching. 'God, I love you, my darling,' Holt muttered against her lips. 'I never thought I'd hear myself say that to any woman and really mean it!' He drew away a little and looked into her eyes. 'When you left Menton the whole place was a howling desert. In three days you'd reduced me to a gibbering idiot!'

'I thought you'd be glad to see me go. You were so beastly to me.'

He gave her a little shake. 'Don't you *see*? The last thing I wanted was to commit myself. I was putting up a fight against falling in love with you from that first moment I set eyes on you.'

The words of the song echoed faintly in Avis's head. 'I took one look at you, that's all I had to do, and then my heart stood still.' So it had happened to him too. It was almost unbelievable.

Holt sank into a chair and pulled her on to his knee, one hand under her thigh, pressing her close against him. 'I told myself I'd get over it, I put up quite a fight, but you were there every moment, I couldn't get you out of my mind.' He grimaced. 'I'd no idea what it was like to fall in love, it was the first time for me. Like getting measles when you're grown up—they say it's always worse.'

He pulled her even closer and his other hand stroked her neck under the heavy fall of pale hair. 'I can't exactly expect you to be in love with me, but for God's sake put me out of my misery and tell me if you're tied up irrevocably with anyone else, so that I can go out and shoot him before I get to work on making you love me!'

He was fooling, but underneath there was the strong thread of sincerity. Avis burrowed her head into his shoulder. 'There *was* Robert,' she said in a small voice, 'but that was in another life, before I met you.'

He was quick on the uptake, he gave a little groan and levered her head up. 'Oh, darling,' he said huskily. For a moment she looked into his eyes, dark and liquid and hypnotic, then his mouth came down on hers, drawing a response from her that became more and more frantic as the kiss went on and on. Her lips parted and every inhibition she had ever had dissolved in a warm tide of desire as Holt's hands moved over her, easing her blouse apart, stroking her shoulder, moving down to cup the softness of her breast, waking sensations that she had never known before—wild, new, erotic stirrings that seemed to make her body separate, an instrument of pleasure.

Somehow, she was hardly aware of it happening, they were lying together on the thick sheepskin rug before the fire and Holt was undressing her with quick, expert movements. A warm, shivering languor took possession of her, and she stretched out her arms and lay back against the roughness of the rug, all thought of resistance gone, revelling in the promise of ecstasy.

The glow of the fire enveloped them both and she saw his face above hers as he leaned on one elbow gazing down at the whiteness of her skin. 'Beautiful—God, you're beautiful,' he murmured brokenly, and she stretched up, smiling, and touched his mouth with one finger, moving her body slowly, instinctively, seductively.

She heard his harsh intake of breath, saw him pull off his shirt, heard the swish of a zip, then he was beside her, one leg thrown across hers, the rough hair of his chest rubbing against her soft, moist skin. As desire mounted she moaned, holding his head in her two hands, drawing it down to her breast while her body arched itself to meet his. She felt his hands moving over her, arousing every nerve-ending, sending her crazy with need, until she breathed aloud, 'I love you, love you,' and felt the weight of his body, taut and hard, on hers.

If there was pain she was unconscious of it in the frenzy of fierce, urgent desire that matched his own as their two bodies twined together, moving as one. Her hands pressed into his spine convulsively and she let out little cries as fulfilment reached the peak of pleasure and heard Holt's groan as he relaxed, rolling away and lying still beside her, his breathing quick and heavy.

Time had ceased to register, but some time later Holt got up and scooped her into his arms and carried her into the bedroom. He laid her on the big bed and covered her lightly with the duvet. Then he shrugged his arms into a crimson silk robe that was lying across a chair and came and looked down at her. 'We never had that tea,' he smiled. 'I'll make some more.'

When he brought the tray back he put it on the bedside table and slipped into bed beside her. The concealed lighting over the bed shone on his dark, tousled hair, and Avis's inside melted with love.

He leaned over and kissed her fleetingly. 'Are you O.K., darling? Warm enough?'

Warm enough! She was glowing all over. She struggled up in bed, pulling the duvet with her. He reached across and pulled it down again, gently. 'Ah, don't cover up, my love. They're gorgeous,' he said, and she giggled as he touched her breasts as if they were some fabulously valuable porcelain. It was wonderful that he had this ability to lighten the situation and not make too solemn a thing of it. Oh, the fun they would have together, she thought with a hazy glimpse into the future. She wouldn't dare to wonder how long it would last.

Holt poured the tea and held out a cup to her. She took it and put it down on her side of the bed. 'I can't sit up drinking tea like this.' She wriggled her shoulders, glancing down at her pearly flesh. 'I'm not used to it. Especially when you're covered up in that dashing red thing.'

He appeared to consider. Then he got up, pulled a black and white striped shirt out of a drawer and tossed it over to her. 'Here you are, then. I want to talk to you, and it might be easier if there wasn't so much of you showing. It rather takes my mind off what I want to say!'

Avis thrust her arms into the shirt and turned up the excess length of the sleeves. Then she settled back with a little sigh against the plump pillows and drank her tea. It tasted as no other tea had ever tasted in her life.

Holt took a cigarette out of a silver case and held it out towards her. She shook her head and he said, 'Do you mind if I do? I don't smoke much—only when I'm panicky about something.'

'*You*—panicky? I don't believe it.'

The lighter flared and he inhaled deeply. 'At this moment,' he confessed, 'I'm far more frightened than when I have to get up in court to defend some villain that I'm damned sure is guilty.'

Avis shook her head helplessly. Then she went cold all over as a horrible thought occurred to her. She rushed into speech before she had time to dwell upon it. 'Are you trying to tell me that now you've—you've had me it's finished and you'd like to get rid of me?' She bit her lip so hard that she tasted blood. 'If that's what it is, I'd—I'd much rather know now.'

Her fingers whitened as they clenched on the handle of the cup. Why had she said that, why had she made it easy for him? she thought despairingly, but she was sure now that she was right. His face didn't give much away, but she thought she could see relief there. She felt suddenly sick. All that talk about love and starting afresh—it was part of his technique. He had wanted to finish what he started in Menton. He had wanted her and he had got her—she had been only too willing.

Gently he prised her tense fingers from the cup and put it down. 'How you do go on!' he said with a grin. 'I never met such a girl for getting on the defensive. What did you say your name meant—"refuge in war", wasn't it? I'm beginning to think it's rather appropriate!'

The grin faded. His face suddenly looked white and strained. 'As a matter of fact,' he said, 'you couldn't be more wrong. Far from wanting to get rid of you I want to keep you. For good,' he added.

Avis went very still. 'You don't mean you want to—to——' She couldn't say the word 'marry', it was too unlikely.

Holt stubbed out the cigarette jerkily and turned towards her, but didn't touch her. 'I mean I'm asking you to marry me—to take me on trust. Can you believe that in spite of all I've said and done in the short time we've known each other I love you to distraction, and I won't get any peace until I've got my ring on your finger.'

'But—but you said you couldn't do with a wife to fuss you and make demands.'

'I said a lot of silly things when we first met. You must try to forget them.'

Avis drew in a long, long breath. Then she drew up the sleeve of the striped shirt and deliberately pinched her forearm.

He watched her, frowning, 'What the hell——' he began.

'I seem to be awake,' she said. 'I thought I must be dreaming.' She lay back against the pillow, trembling inside with shock and delight.

'Well?' He spoke with a hint of his old arrogance, but she saw that his hands were shaking. 'What do you say?'

'Yes,' she said. 'Oh yes, please, Holt!'

He gave a whoop of satisfaction and pulled her into his arms in a bear-hug. Then he held her away and looked deep into her eyes. 'You won't regret it, I swear, my darling. I'll make you happy, we'll have a good life together.' There was a profound sincerity in his voice and Avis gloried in it. This was what she had always dreamed of—this was love.

He drew her closer and said, 'I don't think I can bear to take you home tonight—does it matter? Is there anyone who would worry? You could phone if you like.'

Avis shook her head. 'There's only Janice left now that Jane is married, and she won't worry. Her latest boy-friend was at the wedding.' She chuckled. 'I'm pretty certain that they'll appreciate having the flat to themselves for the night. Anyway, she'll be delighted that I've joined the club.'

He was lying beside her now, his hands wandering over her in a leisurely way. 'Club?' he murmured. 'What club?'

She shivered as his fingers found a sensitive spot at the back of her neck. Then she chuckled again. 'She thought it was almost indecent to be a virgin at my age. She couldn't understand why I wanted to wait.'

'And why did you?' he asked casually. 'Don't tell me if you don't want to.'

'I decided to wait until I fell in love,' said Avis simply. 'And I did wait.'

'Oh, darling,' he groaned, 'I don't deserve you! And that's the nicest compliment I ever had.' He twisted a strand of her hair thoughtfully. 'You do believe I love you, don't you? You're not still remembering how I was at first?'

'I believe you,' she told him, 'and I only remember nice things.'

He eased himself up in the big bed, releasing the girdle of his silk robe and pushing it to the floor, where it fell with a soft swish. Then he reached for her and pulled off the shirt he had lent her. 'Start remembering now,' he said huskily, and drew her into his arms again.

The sunlight was glittering between the long

curtains when Avis awoke. Holt was still asleep, his hair dark against the whiteness of the pillow, and one arm was thrown over her, heavy on her body. She melted with love for him as she lay remembering, savouring every tiny detail of their lovemaking with a dreamy bliss. The miracle had happened. Holt loved her and wanted to marry her, and she was deliriously, ecstatically happy. She stretched her arms above her head as if she would embrace the whole world.

Beside her, Holt wakened and they smiled slowly at each other. Then Avis caught sight of the clock on the table behind his head. 'Heavens, I must get cracking! I must be at the office by half-past nine and I've got to go back to the flat first and pick up something to wear and——'

He pulled himself up lazily and reached for her, but she evaded him and slid out of bed. 'I'll borrow your robe,' she said, picking it up and winding it round her naked body. The silk was smooth and cool against her skin. 'Where's the shower room, and what do you eat for breakfast?'

He guffawed with laughter. 'A practical wife you're going to be, I can see that!'

By a quarter to nine she had showered, dressed once again in the cream silk suit with the pink-striped blouse and done the best she could with the make-up in her handbag. In the tiny kitchen she found milk, a jar of instant coffee, bread and butter and a pot of Oxford marmalade. By the time Holt had showered and dressed the smell of coffee and toast was wafting temptingly through the flat. Avis lifted her eyes from the toaster as he came into the kitchen, and she felt quite faint with love as she saw him leaning against the doorpost looking fabulous in a dark blue suit with a white shirt and a paisley tie.

She pulled herself together. 'Where do you have breakfast usually?'

He grinned and came purposefully towards her. 'Usually—standing up at the sink,' he admitted, glancing through the doorway to where Avis had set a small table by the window in the big living-room, where the sun was slanting in. 'But I can see I shall have to live in a civilised fashion from now on.' He put an arm round her shoulders and kissed the tip of one ear, and she shivered and shook him off when he would have pulled her closer.

'We must be sensible,' she said. 'The world's work must go on.'

'Seems a pity, but I suppose you're right.' Holt sighed, sat down at the table and helped himself to toast and marmalade. 'Let's eat then, and after that I'll drive you back to your flat, if that's what you want. You can pick up a few things that you'll need immediately and put them in the car while we're there. I'm working at home today, I can bring them back with me.'

'But——' Avis puckered her brow, 'I shan't be leaving my flat just yet, shall I?'

'Of course you will, we're going to get married.' His voice was bland, masterful.

'Yes, but—but there are things to arrange—it'll take a while. There's your mother and your family—and I expect my mother will want to fly over for the wedding. And there's my job——'

He leaned over and covered her hand strongly with his. 'Listen, my darling. I've got a big case coming on, starting next week. It's going to be pretty gruelling and it may go on for quite a time. I want to go into it knowing that you'll be there when I come home, knowing that you're my wife. I want us to be married straight away—I believe it only takes a couple of days to arrange.'

'Days!' echoed Avis blankly. To her a wedding was something you planned for weeks in advance, enjoying every exciting detail, choosing clothes, flowers, sending out invitations, planning the reception, the cake. Even her mother's wedding had been quite an event to remember. 'But that wouldn't give people time to make arrangements to come!'

'That,' he said drily, 'is what I was getting at. The fact is that I simply haven't the time to get involved in all the trimmings of a wedding just now and I'm not prepared to wait until the time is right. It might take weeks, and I can't wait that long for you. I need you now.'

'But—but won't they be awfully hurt?' Avis bit her lip.

'They won't know,' he said. 'We'll keep it to ourselves at first, just between the two of us. Later on we could arrange a family get-together—I want very much to meet your mother. But for now— we'll do it my way. Yes?'

He got up and stood behind her chair, drawing her head back against him, his hands slipping from her shoulders to close over her breasts. She felt their touch like an electric current starting a quiver that ran down to her toes.

'Yes?' he whispered in her ear. 'Don't you want us to be married?'

Avis turned her head and met the dark eyes smiling into hers, saw the quirk of his brows, the humorous pull of his lips, and her love for him overflowed. She could deny him nothing. 'Yes,' she said, her eyes brilliant, 'more than anything in the world.'

Avis called in at her flat after she finished work that evening. She had been a little worried about leaving Janice in the lurch.

She sat on the edge of the kitchen table while Janice consumed a slice of quiche. 'The rent's paid up to the end of next month,' she said. 'And of course I'll chip in if you don't find anyone else to share with before then.'

'No problem,' Janice assured her. 'I may not be here much longer myself. The Sainsbury's delicatessen department is thriving,' she added with her wicked little grin.

She put her head on one side. 'So—you're moving in with that heavenly sexy man you brought here this morning? Nice work, you lucky old thing!' She rolled her baby blue eyes. 'You did find romance on the Riviera after all.'

Avis helped herself to a salted peanut from the bowl on the table. 'I suppose you could say that.' More than romance, she thought, she had found love, and that included everything else. Love and marriage. In the words of the song, they went together like a horse and carriage. The old songs had all the best words, she thought, smiling to herself.

If she had been concerned about letting Janice down, she was even more concerned about not telling Mr Hanworthy what she intended doing. She supposed she could have told him the truth, but somewhere deep inside her lurked a suspicion that he might not approve, that he might think it was all too quick, and that he might try to dissuade her. Since her mother left, he had gradually established himself as a kind of father-figure in her life, and she felt she was deceiving him. That hurt a little.

But she was too much in love to allow anything

to spoil her rosy dream-come-true. For three days she floated inches above the ground, doing her work conscientiously in the daytime, because she couldn't do it any other way, and returning to Holt's flat in the evening to cook them a light meal.

He was working desperately hard on his brief. 'Don't take any notice if I'm hard to live with for a day or two,' he told her, flashing her the quick, intimate smile that she loved. 'It'll be better when the case actually starts. It's this weighing everything up beforehand and trying to get some sense out of witnesses that takes years off one's life. It's an embezzlement case and there's big money involved. You have to keep all your wits about you.'

Avis reached up and kissed him swiftly. 'Don't worry, I understand, and I can amuse myself,' she told him, and he shook his head with a kind of wonder and said, 'I'm getting myself the perfect wife!'

After they had eaten he spread his papers on the table and worked far into the night. There was a TV set in the bedroom, and Avis closed the door and turned the sound volume down and passed the evening pleasantly enough. They shared a bed, but after that first night Holt didn't make love to her again. Each night it was after three o'clock when he finally crept into bed and fell into a deep sleep. Avis slept very lightly—she was too excited by everything that was happening to relax completely—and she heard him tiptoe into the darkened bedroom, felt the springs of the mattress sag under his weight, listened to his deep sigh of exhaustion before he fell asleep. After that she slept herself, a little smile on her lips.

On Friday they were married. Avis took half an hour extra on her lunch time in order to get into town by taxi, and they met at the Registrar's office. She wore her ordinary neat brown business suit, with a new champagne-coloured blouse with ruffles at the neck. 'My one bit of bridal finery,' she laughed when Holt pinned a creamy rosebud to her lapel in the waiting-room.

'You're a wonderful girl and I adore you,' he said softly, just before the clerk called them in. 'Thank you for being so understanding. Later on, we'll have a real slap-up do, and you shall buy all the new clothes you fancy.'

There was no wedding lunch. After the short, dry ceremony with two young clerks brought in as witnesses, there was only time for a drink and a sandwich standing up in a crowded bar in Fleet Street before Avis had to get a taxi back to work and Holt had to return to his chambers. 'Bless you,' he said, closing the taxi door. The taxi was caught in traffic and Avis sat and watched the tall straight form as he hurried away from her along the crowded pavement and disappeared among the crowd. Just for a moment she felt a little wave of uneasiness. Then she touched the bright new gold ring on her finger and the feeling passed. There was so much to look forward to, so much to plan, so much happiness ahead.

She told Mr Hanworthy that afternoon, when she took his cup of tea in to him during a slack moment between clients' appointments.

'Married?' His cup clattered into its saucer. 'Did you say *married*? Well, well, well, this is a bolt from the blue! Is it—could it be young Holt Clavell? Yes, I see I'm right. No prizes for guessing. I saw your face when he called in the other day, my dear. You'd had a lovers' tiff in France and now it's all come right, is that it?'

'Er—something like that,' Avis murmured.

Mr Hanworthy smiled his benign smile. 'You young people, you can't wait, can you? Now in my day we planned a wedding months ahead. Still, times change, and I'm very happy for you. Clavell—yes, a clever young man, he'll go far. Good family—they have a nice place up in the Cotswolds, I expect you've been there. There was something in his father's will——' he rubbed his chin thoughtfully '—I don't recall at the moment. Now then, we must celebrate the occasion. Send Jessica out to buy a cake. I have a bottle of sherry. At the end of the afternoon we'll all foregather and drink to your happiness! Suddenly he looked alarmed. 'You won't be leaving me straight away, will you, Avis?'

She shook her head, smiling. 'No, of course not. I'll wait until there's someone to take my place. If you decide on one of the other girls I could be showing her the ropes.' She hadn't thought to ask Holt if he wanted her to give up her job. She hadn't had a chance to talk to him about their life together. She didn't even know where she would be living—she supposed in London. Possibly he went to the Cotswolds at weekends or when he had spare time. A tiny frown furrowed her forehead. She really didn't know anything at all about him, did she? Again that faint uneasiness stirred, but she pushed it away quickly and went to tell Jessica about the cake.

Going back to the flat she struck the rush-hour, but even so she was in before Holt. She busied herself tidying up and preparing a meal to heat in the microwave. She had bought a ham-and-mushroom quiche, with which she planned to serve a fabulous salad with nuts and raisins, and crusty new rolls and some of Holt's favourite Stilton to follow, with ice-cream for herself. She was learning Holt's favourite preferences in food by degrees, but cooking facilities in the flat were limited to the microwave oven, an electric kettle, a toaster and a coffee-maker. Bachelor stuff. Perhaps soon she would have a real kitchen to cook in, but she would have to wait and see what Holt suggested. For the moment it was enough that she was his wife and able to help him through this period of pressure in his work and not worry him about domestic matters.

It was a chilly evening and she set the small table in front of the electric fire, with primroses in a little blue pot in the centre. She took time over the salad and when it was finished it looked almost as good as an illustration from one of the glossy cookery books. She regarded it with satisfaction; after all, this *was* a kind of wedding breakfast. Holt could take an hour or so off from his work on this special evening, surely?

After dinner—it would be morning in Adelaide—they had planned to telephone her mother. Avis felt churned up when she thought of that phone call. Her mother would be happy for her, she was sure of that, but perhaps a little hurt that she hadn't been told before the wedding. Perhaps a little worried that it had all been so quick and unexpected.

She went into the bedroom and changed into her prettiest dress—a cinnamon brown angora wool with a gathered skirt and a low, cowl neckline. She brushed her hair until it fell like a shining curtain to her creamy shoulders. She dusted her eyelids with her new bronze shadow. It made her look different, more sophisticated, more—sexy. She giggled unsteadily as her eyes turned to the big bed with its plump downy cover. Tonight, surely, they would make love again.

She felt a warm stirring inside and went quickly back to the kitchen to set up the coffee machine.

It was nearly nine when Holt finally came in. He kissed her absently, dropped into a chair and closed his eyes. Avis mixed him a whisky—by now she knew exactly how he liked it.

He nodded his thanks and tossed off the drink. 'I'll be human in a few minutes. It's been a God-awful afternoon. Benton turned up with a whole set of new ledgers that he'd "forgotten" about.' He rolled his lips sarcastically around the word. 'I had to start all over again. Why didn't I specialise in something simple like divorce or larceny?' He pulled himself out of the chair. 'I'll have a shower and then I'm afraid I'll have to get going again. I've brought the lot back with me.' He pointed to a bulging briefcase on the floor beside him.

'But you'll have a meal?' Avis hovered anxiously on her way to the kitchen. Had he forggoten that it was their wedding day? He hadn't even mentioned it.

'No, thanks, I sent out for something on a tray only about an hour ago. I might have a sandwich and coffee later on.' He disappeared into the bedroom.

Avis cleared the table and put it ready for Holt to work on. In the kitchen she poured out a cup of black coffee and drank it. It was very strong— Holt liked his coffee strong and black—and it tasted bitter. She pressed her lips together to stop them trembling. She remembered so vividly what he had said in Menton, that at present his career must come first and that to have a wife fussing and making demands would be the height of folly. I *won't* be a demanding wife, she told herself. I'll try to understand and make allowances. But she felt empty inside and her throat ached from controlling the tears. Not for the first time she wished she was one of those girls who didn't weep so easily.

She didn't bother with the quiche. She spooned some salad on to a plate with a wedge of cheese and a hunk of bread and ate it from a tray in front of the fire while Holt pored over his work. He seemed not to notice her presence, and that was good, she told herself. It meant that there was a sympathy between them already if he could forget about her while he was working. But she looked at his dark head, bent over the heavy books, his long legs stretched out beneath the table, and the ache inside her got so unbearable that presently she went into the bedroom and switched on the TV and tried unsuccessfully to get involved in an old Fred Astaire film.

When the programme was over she went through to the kitchen and made more coffee and cut sandwiches, using the cheese that was to have been part of their wedding dinner. She took the tray into the living room and put it on the low table by the fire.

Holt raised his eyes from his work after a moment or two. He looked desperately tired; the thick-fringed lids drooped and there were dark lines under his eyes. 'I'm not being very good company, am I?' he said wryly. 'This is how it is sometimes, I'm afraid. Think you can stick it?'

'I expect so,' she said in a practical tone. She poured coffee and took it to him, with the plate of sandwiches. She wanted to say, 'How much longer will you be?' and, 'You look tired out, shouldn't you pack it in now?' She longed to put her arms around him and tell him she loved him. But she saw his eyes going back to his work as he munched a sandwich.

He said, 'This is going to be a long job, darling. You'd better go off to bed.'

Just as it had been for the last two nights. And had he forgotten they were going to ring her mother in Adelaide? But tomorrow would do just as well, she told herself firmly. 'O.K.,' she said, producing a yawn. 'I am a bit tired.' She bent and put a hand on his shoulder and kissed his cheek. 'Goodnight, Holt dear.'

He turned his head and looked up into her eyes with an odd expression, and for a moment she thought he was going to reach up and pull her down into his arms. Oh, let him do that, she prayed. Let him kiss me and tell me he loves me.

But her prayer wasn't answered. He reached up and patted her hand lightly. 'You're very long-suffering, darling. This isn't much of a wedding night for you, is it? We'll make up for it later on, I promise you. When this case is over we might have a weekend at the cottage in the Cotswolds.'

Avis went to bed a little happier. At least he had remembered that it was their wedding night. She slipped into the shimmering scrap of white chiffon and lace that she had bought specially for tonight and stood before the long mirror remembering the night they had made love. A warm tide of desire began to rise inside her and grip her with an aching need.

She got into bed, but it was impossible to lie still and compose herself for sleep, and she crept out again and padded up and down the room, her toes curling into the thick, soft carpet. Every nerve felt raw and quivering. Never before had she been so aware of her own body and its needs.

She stood beside the closed door, digging her fingernails into her palms. She must go to him, she must. Would his face soften into love or would he merely look faintly bored? Oh God, she moaned aloud, I want him so much, want his arms round

me, the weight of his body on mine. The longing
was sending her crazy.

She turned the door-handle, and at the same
moment the phone buzzed in the next room. She
heard Holt's voice, then a long silence, then he
spoke again. She couldn't hear the words, and his
tone told her nothing. The conversation went on
and on; she could almost imagine he was arguing
about something. Then at last the extension phone
beside the bed gave a click and she knew he had
rung off. She slipped back into bed, quickly, not
knowing what to expect, and picked up a book.

Presently the bedroom door opened softly and
Holt put his head round it. 'Ah, you're not asleep
yet.' He came over and sat on the edge of the bed,
his shoulders sagging with weariness.

'That was Mama.' He lifted his eyes to the
ceiling and clicked his tongue. 'Oh dear, oh dear,
she's well and truly got the wind up about herself
this time! Hadn't meant to ring me at this hour of
the night, but she couldn't sleep and she was quite
obviously really wrought up, poor darling. The
gist of it is that she's started to imagine all sorts of
awful things about her health and she wants to
come back to England to see Dr Trimley—her
specialist here. To complicate matters my brother
Peter's wife has turned up and parked herself on
Mama. They—er—don't get on, as you'll find out
when you know our family a little better.'

Avis nodded quietly. 'I rather gathered that,
from something your mother said——'

'Yes—well, the upshot is that Hazel has decided
to stay for three weeks, and Mama is understand-
ably appalled at the idea. Five minutes of Hazel
is quite enough, and the prospect of being, as she
says, bossed around all day is sending poor Mama
quietly mad. She rang up to ask if I could possibly

spare the time to go down and escort her back
home myself.'

There was a short silence. He ran his fingers
distractedly through his thick dark hair. 'It was the
very devil trying to explain that I couldn't go, not
with this big case coming on. I'm sure she's
worrying quite unnecessarily about herself, but
that's beside the point, and I wouldn't hurt her for
the world.'

Another silence. 'So, what did you say?' Avis
prompted.

Holt raised his head and gave her an apologetic
little smile. 'I told her you would go,' he said. 'Do
you mind? It would be a kind act, she likes you.
And you're one of the family now, aren't you, my
sweet?'

He leaned forward and took both her hands in
his. 'This isn't a very romantic start to a
honeymoon, is it? First I leave you by yourself
while I'm engulfed in work, then I send you
hareing off to the other side of Europe to look
after my mama.' His face softened into a smile.
'And you're looking so bewitching too, my poor
darling.' He touched the froth of lace at her neck
with one finger.

For a moment she thought he would move
nearer to take her in his arms, and she held her
breath, willing him to do just that. But instead,
with a wry grimace he dropped his hand and said,
'But I must resist temptation and live a monklike
existence until this case is over. That's something
I've had to school myself to do before.'

Avis's stomach clenched. He couldn't have
made it clearer—she was just one of a long string
of women he had made love to when he had
time—and whom he could resist just as easily
when his work demanded it. There was the

difference that she was his wife, of course, but for an empty, desolate moment she wondered why he had bothered to marry her.

She said, 'Did you tell your mother that we're married?'

He looked at her a little curiously. Perhaps her tone had told him something of what she was feeling. 'No,' he said. 'I thought it better not to tell her on the phone—she'd stay awake for the rest of the night, thinking about it. You tell her when you get there. I promise she'll be delighted,' he added with an amused lift of his eyebrows.

Again Avis had the uneasy feeling that there was something here she didn't understand, but she pushed it away. 'What about the office?' she asked. 'I told Mr Hanworthy I'd be coming in tomorrow morning.'

'I'll get in touch with him myself and explain,' Holt told her offhandedly.

He stopped and turned on his way back to the door. 'Do you mind going?' he queried, and she gave him the answer he so obviously expected.

'No, of course I don't mind. I'll see about getting a flight first thing in the morning.'

'That's my girl,' he said absently, and she could see his mind had gone back to his work even before he went out of the bedroom and closed the door.

Avis was feeling strung up and apprehensive when she finally arrived at the white villa up in the hills above Menton, some thirty-six hours later. She didn't know what to expect, and Holt had been vague and preoccupied when she tried to ask him questions. 'You'll have to judge the situation when you get there,' he had said maddeningly. 'Get a taxi from the airport—we won't announce your coming, that might complicate matters, with dear Hazel in residence. You'll appreciate what I mean when you see her,' he added with a grimace.

This time there was no leisurely approach to the house, as she had had with Jacques driving. The taxi from the airport at Nice whisked her at an alarming speed along a motorway, and when she had paid the driver and climbed the steps to the front door of the villa she was feeling tense with stress added to stress.

Marie opened the door and seemed delighted as she beamed, *'Bonjour*, Mademoiselle Brown, *comment allez-vous?'* and took her travelling bag.

'Madame Clavell?' Avis enquired. She remembered that Marie spoke no English.

'Yes? Who wants me?' a woman's voice said sharply. Marie and Avis turned together in the direction of the drawing-room door. Then Marie shrugged with an old-fashioned glance towards Avis, and hurried away upstairs with the travelling bag.

Avis stood where she was as the speaker approached. She was about thirty, dressed in a slate-grey suit with pearls round her neck. Pale hair, pale eyes; pale skin. There was no colour about her anywhere.

'I take it you're the girl that my brother-in-law has sent?' She looked Avis up and down. 'Although I really can't imagine why,' she added sourly.

This was evidently Hazel, and Avis found herself disliking the woman on sight—her tight mouth, her supercilious manner. But Hazel was part of her new family now, and Avis didn't intend to start off by making an enemy of her if she could help it.

'Holt is madly busy just now,' she said

pleasantly. 'He has a case coming into court in a couple of days, and he knew his mother would understand that he couldn't get down to see her himself. How is she today? Perhaps I could see her straight away?'

'Certainly not,' the woman said sharply. 'My mother-in-law is in bed and she's not well enough to see strangers. If you have any messages from her son please give them to me.'

This was going to be difficult. Avis wished Holt had told his mother about their marriage and not left it to her. The sooner she broke the news the better.

'I would like to see her myself,' she said quietly. 'I'll go up to her room—I know my way from the last time I was here.'

She turned towards the stairs, but Hazel stepped in front of her, barring her way. 'Such impertinence!' she snapped. 'I won't have an office girl coming here and upsetting Mrs Clavell! Kindly wait here in the hall while I go up and see her.' She put out a hand as if she were expecting Avis to squeeze past her, and delivered what amounted to a push backwards.

Avis stumbled and recovered her balance. Anger simmered inside her, but she managed to hold on to her temper. 'Please let me pass,' she said, 'I have every bit as much right to see Mrs Clavell as you have. She's *my* mother-in-law too, you know. Holt and I were married yesterday.'

The effect of her announcement was astounding. Hazel's mouth fell open and the blood drained from her face, leaving it a dirty grey colour. The pale eyes stared wildly at Avis as if she had delivered a death sentence. At last the woman spluttered, 'I don't believe it. You're lying!' Two patches of crimson appeared on her cheeks. 'Yes, that's what it is, you're trying to get the better of me. You're just a lying little bitch, like all your kind!'

Avis was cold with shock. She hadn't expected to be welcomed into the family with open arms by her new sister-in-law; she had received the impression from both Mrs Clavell and from Holt that Peter's wife wasn't the affectionate type. But she certainly hadn't expected this hysterical reaction.

'Why should I lie?' she said calmly, and held out her left hand with the shining new wedding ring on it.

Hazel stared at her hand as if it were a poisonous snake. Then, with a strangled sound in her throat, she turned away and stumbled into the drawing room, slamming the door behind her.

Avis was trembling all over. What was happening, and what sort of a situation had she got herself into with the Clavell family? Again she was conscious of a feeling of uneasiness and foreboding. Before, it had only been fleeting and had passed away almost immediately. But this time it came down like a dark cloud all around her.

Very slowly, holding on to the banisters, she walked up the stairs to Mrs Clavell's room.

CHAPTER SEVEN

Avis's inside twisted with compassion when she saw Mrs Clavell. She was in bed, lying propped up by pillows, and she looked very ill, her face haggard and great dark smudges under her eyes. It seemed to make it worse that she was still, in a poignant way, so very beautiful, like a rose battered by a storm.

But her face brightened as Avis came into the room, the smoky grey eyes glowed in the light that filtered between the drawn curtains. 'Avis—my dear girl, you've really come! Holt said he would send you to me, but I hardly dared to believe it. I've felt so wretchedly alone.' Her eyes filled with weak tears and she groped under the pillow for her handkerchief. She held out a hand and Avis went across the room and sat on the bed, taking the limp hand between her own strong young fingers.

'Holt was so worried that he couldn't come himself.' That wasn't quite true, but Avis was sure that if he could see his mother now he wouldn't doubt that she was really ill. 'He's bogged down with work—you know, this case that's coming on in a couple of days. So he asked me if I'd come instead.'

Mrs Clavell wiped her eyes with shaking hands. 'Silly of me to give way like this,' she murmured, 'but I was so relieved to see you. I'd been feeling so rotten, and then Hazel turned up.' She grimaced. 'And *that* didn't do me any good! She tried to jolly me along and I don't feel a bit jolly.'

She cast an anxious glance towards the door. 'Have you seen her since you arrived?'

'Yes—we introduced ourselves. I—er—got the impression that she didn't approve of me.'

'Hazel,' said Mrs Clavell, 'isn't a very approving sort of person.' She met Avis's eyes with a glimmer of a smile. 'Am I a very horrid, critical mother-in-law?'

This was Avis's cue. 'I'm sure you're a wonderful mother-in-law.' She gripped Mrs Clavell's hand a little more tightly. 'Can you bear a bit of a shock?' she asked.

Mrs Clavell's free hand clutched the bedcover. 'It's not Holt? He's not ill? Had an accident? Is that why he——'

'No, nothing like that. Holt's fine,' Avis hastened to reassure her. 'It's just that he—I—oh well, there's no way of breaking the news gently. We were married yesterday morning.'

There was a stunned silence in the room, and Avis watched Mrs Clavell's face anxiously. Her reaction was almost as unexpected as Hazel's had been, although very different. It was like a slow-motion picture. Her face crumpled, then the tears flooded into her eyes and trickled down her cheeks. 'Do you mind—are you disappointed?' Avis surveyed her worriedly.

'*Mind? Disappointed?*' the older woman gulped helplessly. She was laughing and crying at the same time. 'My dear, dear girl, I'm delighted and relieved. You've no idea what this means to me. It's wonderful, wonderful news!' She drew Avis into her arms and kissed her. 'It isn't altogether a surprise, although I never dreamed it would happen so quickly.'

Avis smiled wryly. 'I think you might say he swept me off my feet.'

'Oh yes, that's so like Holt. He thinks things out first, but when he makes up his mind he loses no time in putting plans into action. But where were you married, and who was there? And what does your dear mother think of it? Tell me all about it.' Her lassitude had disappeared. She was wide awake now.

It wasn't easy, but Avis did her best to paint a picture that was much more colourful than the actual wedding had been. 'But registrars' offices aren't the most romantic of places, are they? Holt promises that we'll have a big party when he gets through this important case, and invite everyone. I'm sure my mother will want to come over from Australia for it.' She couldn't admit that her mother hadn't even been told of the marriage yet. That would seem to put Holt in a bad light, and she wouldn't want to do that. *She* understood that his work had to come first just now, even before his new bride, but not everyone might understand, not even his mother.

'That will be splendid,' Mrs Clavell said, but Avis heard a wistful note in her voice. 'You must have the party at Dell Cottage, we have so many old friends in the Cotswolds and Holt grew up there. I just hope——' She broke off, looking out of the window, and her body sagged against the pillows.

Then she seemed to gain energy and pulled herself up again. 'Now I'm going to ask you something, Avis dear. I really have been feeling rather wretched lately and I'm sure I'd be better back in England. I have my own specialist there and I'd like very much to consult him. It isn't that I don't trust Doctor Jago, but—well, as I told you before I don't find her particularly *sympathique*. I've had the impression that she's been more interested in meeting my son here than in diagnosing my ailments.' She pulled a wry face that took the sting of criticism from the words.

Avis nodded, remembering her own jealous pangs when Hélène Jago's black eyes had flashed an unmistakable message to Holt.

'Well, finally I decided to get a second opinion and called in another local doctor. He seemed to think I should go into hospital for tests straight away. He was very definite about it and talked about a possible operation—I think he was trying to prepare me.' Her face puckered. 'I'm an awful baby about hospitals, and if I've got to have something done I must be at home in England, in the care of my own specialist. You do understand, don't you, my dear?' she added with an anxious look at Avis.

'Of course I do, and I'm sure you're right. You'll feel much happier within reach of a specialist, you know. Would you like me to arrange the journey for you? I'm sure that's what Holt would wish, but I could perhaps phone him first to let him know what's happening. He asked me to do that.'

Actually, he hadn't. It had been after three this morning when he finally got into bed beside her and she had pretended to be asleep. He was asleep himself almost immediately, breathing evenly and quietly. Avis crushed down the nagging little hurt that he hadn't even noticed she was in the bed with him.

This morning she had got up and dressed early and he hadn't wakened. She had done all the telephoning and arranged her flight and set the table for his breakfast before he emerged, heavy-eyed and badly needing a shave.

'Everything's laid on,' she said brightly. 'Coffee's

ready when you want it. I've booked a taxi to take me to Heathrow, is that O.K.? I'll phone you when I get to Menton, shall I, and let you know how your mother is?'

He gave her a twisted smile. 'The perfect secretary as well as the perfect wife! What a lucky man I am!' But she saw his eyes go to his briefcase, propped up against the table.

She looked out of the window. 'Mind you remember that!' she teased. 'Here's my cab now, I'll be off.'

As he moved with her towards the door she said, 'No, don't bother to come down with me, I'm travelling very light.' She picked up the small satchel into which she had managed to cram everything she would need for a couple of nights—for she didn't intend to stay any longer than that whatever happened—and gave him a quick kiss that landed just above his ear. 'Goodbye, Holt dear, I hope all goes well with the case.'

A wifely little speech, she thought, as she ran down the stairs to the waiting taxi, but it had sounded stiff and false. The trouble was that she didn't feel like Holt's wife—not yet.

But not for the world would she let Mrs Clavell guess that she had even the faintest doubts, and now when her new mother-in-law gave her a knowing little smile and said, 'We must get back as soon as possible. I know Holt won't want to let you out of his sight for a moment longer than necessary,' she even felt herself blush.

'I'll go down and try to get through to him now,' she said. 'And then I'll ring the airport and see about getting a flight for us.' She hesitated. 'Is—is Hazel coming too?'

Mrs Clavell lifted her eyes to the ceiling. 'Heaven preserve us! No, I don't imagine so. She makes a habit of giving herself little holidays down here on her own quite often, leaving the boys to a nanny. I don't like to admit it, but I fear that Peter is quite glad to let her come without him.' She sighed and her eyes clouded; then she smiled again. 'Never mind, I have you now, Avis my dear, and I'll try not to be a burden to you. Yes, you go and ring Holt—the telephone's in the hall. Tell him how delighted I am about your news and how I'm looking forward to seeing him.'

Avis went out and closed the door. She was halfway down the stairs before she realised that the door of the cloakroom was wide open and Hazel was already speaking on the phone in there. Her high, petulant tones carried easily upwards.

Avis hesitated, half turning to go back, not wanting to encounter Hazel again nor to listen to a private conversation. Then she stopped as she caught the words '—yes, my dear Leonie, I'm afraid it's true. He's married a cheap little office typist. She's just turned up, looking like a cat with a saucer of cream and waving a wedding ring in my face.' A pause. 'You didn't know this was on the cards, he didn't tell you? Well, I think that was cruel, but you know how impossible Holt can be at times. No, of course it won't last—don't worry, he'll be back with you in no time, this chit of a girl couldn't hold him. What? Well, of course it's quite obvious. As things are, he had to marry *somebody* straight away. What a tragedy your divorce is so long in coming through. What? The cottage? Yes, I'm afraid it puts paid to all that as far as Peter and I are concerned. It will go to Holt now that he's got himself a wife—I could murder him for it! But I don't want to talk about that side of it, I'm absolutely *shattered*—yes, I'll see you when I get

back in a week or two. I haven't the heart to cope
with the brats again just yet. Goodbye, Leonie.'

Avis stood rigid, her hand locked round the
banister. Then she went slowly downstairs.

Hazel was crossing the hall and they met face to
face. Hazel's sallow cheeks reddened and for a
moment she looked embarrassed, but she recovered
immediately. 'So—you were listening to that, were
you? And did you like what you heard?' she
sneered. 'Did it please you to hear that your
darling husband is hardly likely to be faithful to
you for long? Did he tell you about all the other
women he's had? Did he tell you why he wanted to
marry you in such a hurry?' The words poured out
in a thin vicious stream.

Avis felt as if she had been kicked in the
stomach. It was a bad dream, it had to be. This
woman was a harpy, one of those evil spirits you
meet in a nightmare. She heard herself say, 'I don't
know what you're talking about.' She wanted to
walk past, but her legs were like lead.

'Don't you indeed?' The other woman was
almost shrieking now. 'Then you'd better ask him.'
The pale eyes narrowed into cunning slits. 'Ask
him why he suddenly wanted to get married so
urgently—*just when he discovered that his mother is
seriously ill.*'

'But he doesn't—I mean, he doesn't think she's
seriously ill. It was only yesterday evening when
she telephoned him——'

'Don't give me that! Of course he knew.' Hazel
spat out the words contemptuously. 'Only a fool
wouldn't know she's really ill, and Holt's no fool.'

Was it true? Had Hélène Jago told him? Had he
seen the new doctor before he left here? Or——?
Avis put a hand against her forehead. She felt like
a poor swimmer in deep, deep water.

'I really don't know what you're talking about. Holt married me because he loves me. Why else should he want to marry me?'

Hazel's thin lips curled. 'What a stupid girl you are! You don't imagine that a sophisticated type like Holt Clavell would fall in love so suddenly with a little nonentity of a typist, do you? Of course he didn't, he was just using you. The truth is that he needed to marry immediately and you were on the spot and ready to jump at the chance. But it won't last, of course, in spite of whatever lies he's told you. It should be quite easy for him to get an annulment, he's a clever bastard and he'll know all the right legal strings to pull. I don't suppose he's had sex with you since the ceremony.'

The woman's face was thrust nearer, and the expression in the pale eyes that peered avidly at Avis made her recoil with disgust. 'He hasn't, has he?' Avis felt her cheeks flame and Hazel added triumphantly, 'There you are, you see!'

Avis's stomach was churning and she was afraid she was going to be sick. 'You're horrible— beastly,' she whispered painfully.

'Oh no, my dear, just realistic. As a matter of fact I feel quite sorry for you, but we all have to grow up at some time. But I really can't be bothered with you any longer,' Hazel added spitefully. 'You'll have to get the rest of the story from that *temporary* husband of yours. Ask him to tell you all about the stupid will his father made.' She flounced away across the hall, then stopped to add vindictively over her shoulder, '*And* about the woman he's been living with for the last six months!'

There was a chair beside the telephone table. Avis sank on to it, her legs buckling under her as if she'd run a marathon. Her heart was racing, her

hands clammy. She knew she was suffering the
physical symptoms of shock, but she knew, too,
that she mustn't let herself think about what had
just taken place. There was *something*—something
that she didn't know about—but Holt would tell
her in his own good time. Meanwhile she would
ignore the beastly insinuations of a spiteful,
venomous woman. Holt loved her, of course he
did. He had told her so and she believed him.

She looked at the telephone. She wouldn't try to
contact him—not now. Not after what Hazel had
just said. All those sly hints and half-statements
had been like poison darts and she must give
herself time to get the poison out of her blood.
Instead she would ring the airport and make
arrangements to get Mrs Clavell back to England—
away from Hazel—at the first possible moment.
For both their sakes.

Holt was waiting for them at Heathrow when they
arrived two days later and drove them straight to
his flat in Chelsea. He was very quiet as the car
threaded its way through the London traffic. Mrs
Clavell was obviously exhausted and Avis had an
odd feeling of unreality—as if all this were
happening to someone else.

At the flat she made Mrs Clavell comfortable
on the sofa in the big living room and went into
the kitchen to make tea. Holt followed her in.
'Mama should go straight to bed,' she said,
'she'll need a good deal of care, she's not at all
well.'

He gave her a clouded look. 'I don't dispute
that—*now*.' He spoke curtly, as if she had
intended to criticise him. 'But you realise that
there's only one bed, don't you?'

'Then she must have that. We'll just have to

manage for tonight. Tomorrow we can make some arrangements.'

He raised dark brows, shrugging. 'I'm in your hands. You're doing the planning.'

'Do you mind?'

'Of course I don't,' he said impatiently. 'I'm very grateful.' He didn't sound particularly grateful, and she couldn't avoid the thought that he wasn't acting or sounding like a man in love who hadn't seen his new wife for three days.

Her hand shook as she poured boiling water into the teapot and a few drops splashed on to her arm. She winced, but Holt didn't notice; he wasn't looking at her. 'I have my uses,' she said rather tartly.

He did look at her then, frowning. 'What the hell does that mean?'

'Nothing,' said Avis. 'Nothing of any consequence.' She picked up the tray and walked past him into the living room. It seemed to her that a high wall was going up between herself and Holt. But there were urgent matters to be attended to in the immediate future and nothing could be said now. Personal matters must take a back seat, and Avis determined to bring all her training to the task of organisation.

And that was exactly what she did for the next days—and crowded days they were. Making appointments with two different specialists, one of them a surgeon; ferrying Mrs Clavell around in taxis—to the hospital for tests and back to the specialists again, and providing moral and physical support as best she could; contacting Holt's brother Peter in Birmingham, after many abortive phone calls; trying to persuade Mrs Clavell to eat some of the light meals she prepared; reading to her to take her mind off the impending results of the tests.

The day following their arrival from Menton the legal case that was so important to Holt came into court, and after that they saw very little of him. When he did put in an appearance now and then, he looked moody and preoccupied.

Avis had looked forward to being a help and comfort to him during the trial. After all, that was why they had married so hastily, wasn't it? *Wasn't it?* 'I want to go into the case knowing that you'll be there when I come home, knowing that you're my wife.' That was what he had said, but things had turned out very differently. He had his meals somewhere else—she didn't know where—and he spent his limited free time sitting with his mother. When he spoke to Avis it was only to enquire about the progress of the medical investigations. Avis knew that he was convinced now that his mother was really ill and not putting on an act, as he had once called it. But he never raised that point and all he said to her was, 'Thank you for taking charge of Mama and seeing her through this, Avis. I'm more grateful than I can say.'

Oh yes, he was grateful, she was sure of that. But there was something missing between them—a closeness should have been growing, instead of which any closeness there had been seemed to have disappeared. They didn't even have a bed to share. Holt wouldn't hear of his mother going to a hotel, as she had suggested. Instead she had the one big bed, Avis slept on the comfortable sofa, and Holt himself stretched out in an armchair when he had put away his papers for the night. 'I can sleep anywhere,' he said carelessly, and Avis couldn't help the treacherous little thought that crept into her mind—anywhere but with your wife.

Then, one afternoon when they had been back

in London just over a week, Avis opened the door to see Dr Trimley, Mrs Clavell's specialist, standing there, and her heart sank. He didn't have the look of a man bearing reassuring news.

'My husband's in court, Dr Trimley,' she told him, leading him into the living-room. 'And my mother-in-law is resting. Will you see her, or——'

The specialist was a large man with a gentle voice and masses of thick grey hair. He settled himself in a chair. 'Not just yet, I think, Mrs Clavell. I'll have a word with you first. No, nothing to drink, thanks.'

Avis perched nervously on the edge of the chair opposite. 'Have you—do you know the results of the tests yet?'

He nodded slowly. 'They were ready this morning when I went into hospital. Mr Lane and I have discussed them thoroughly.' Mr Lane was the surgeon. 'I won't beat about the bush, Mrs Clavell. We want your mother-in-law in hospital immediately.'

Avis felt suddenly cold. 'Then—then it's serious?'

The big man sat forward in his chair and his eyes were kind. 'I can put it to you straight, can't I, Mrs Clavell? We believe your mother-in-law has a rather rare metabolic condition which has probably been coming on for years. It's impossible to say precisely how far advanced it is until we operate. All I can tell you at this stage is that if we don't take it in time and the condition blows up suddenly, it would certainly be very serious indeed. I won't go into all the details with you, but I felt you should know the situation. You've been a comfort and support to your mother-in-law recently, I've seen that.'

'I'm very fond of her,' said Avis in a low

voice. 'Will you see her now and break the news to her?'

He nodded and stood up. 'I shall, naturally, be tactful,' he said gently. 'Mrs Clavell is a somewhat highly-strung lady, but in my experience it's often her type who faces up well to difficult situations. I should like to see your husband as soon as possible—would you ask him to telephone me— I'll leave you my home address to contact if he can't get me at my consulting rooms. Meanwhile, perhaps you could see that Mrs Clavell comes into hospital straight away—today. I'll make all the necessary arrangements at that end. This is where you come to.' He scribbled on a pad, tore off a sheet and gave it to her.

Over and over again, for the rest of that day, Avis thought that the specialist had been right. Mrs Clavell was wonderful. In the taxi that took them to the hospital she looked almost contented. 'It's a relief to know that something is being done,' she said to Avis with her wry little smile. 'I've thought for ages that there was something wrong, but it never really flared up, and I knew everyone thought I was imagining it. Everyone but you, my dear child.' She put a hand affectionately over Avis's. 'You're a kind, sensitive girl and you've been very good to me over the last rather difficult days. Holt is a lucky man to have you.'

Avis smiled mistily, but could find nothing to say.

Holt returned earlier than usual that evening. Avis told him the news immediately and left him to telephone the specialist while she went into the kitchen to get ham and cheese and salad out of the fridge, just in case he wanted a meal quickly. When she went back into the living room he was sitting beside the telephone table, his dark head resting on his hands, in an attitude of utter dejection, and her heart melted. She went over and put her arm round his shoulders, resting her cheek against his hair. 'She's going to come through, darling,' she said softly. 'I'm sure she is.'

He stood up, turning away from her, and her hands fell to her side. 'I'm going to the hospital straight away,' he said. She might not have spoken. He didn't want any comfort or love from her, that was all too evident.

In a choky little voice, Avis said, 'Yes, of course.' She felt cold all through.

'I don't know when I'll be back,' he said, and went out and slammed the door as if he were in a rage about something.

It was the longest, most miserable evening and night that Avis had ever spent in her life. Many times she went to the phone to ring the hospital—but what could they tell her? She turned on the TV and stared unseeingly at it for a few minutes, then switched it off again. She picked up the evening newspaper that Holt had brought in with him and read about the case he was engaged in. But it was too complicated for her to follow in her present state of mind.

When Holt hadn't come back by midnight she went to bed and tried not to worry. That night she had, perhaps, an hour's sleep in all, and she was thankful when it was light and she could get up and make tea and occupy herself tidying the flat.

Holt came in at half-past eight. He stood inside the door, staring at her. He looked dreadful. The question was in her eyes, but she didn't speak. 'They've done more tests,' he said tersely, 'and the situation's even worse than they thought. They're operating this morning.' He looked away. 'It seems she has a fifty-fifty chance—or somewhat less.' And before Avis could say a word he went into the bathroom and she heard the rush of the shower.

Avis made toast and coffee. When Holt emerged from the bedroom, he was dressed immaculately in a dark blue suit. His hair was gleaming wetly from his shower, his face was grey with fatigue and he had cut himself shaving. Her heart ached for him. If only he would talk to her, let her share with him as a wife should. But his face was grim and forbidding. He was miles away from her.

He tossed down a cup of black coffee standing up, then reached for his briefcase. 'I've arranged to stay with a colleague until the trial's over,' he said. 'It's nearer the hospital and it will save time travelling across town.' He threw a wad of notes down on the table. 'You can keep things ticking over here, can't you?'

'Yes, of course,' said Avis in a small, muffled voice. She passed a hand over her forehead. 'What would be best for me to do today? Shall I go to the hospital? They might let me see Mama when she comes round from the anaesthetic, and it would be reassuring for her if there was one of us there.'

Holt stood by the door, looking down at her, and suddenly she felt about two inches high. For what seemed an eternity he stared at her, his face completely expressionless. Then he turned away. 'Do what you bloody well like!' he shouted, then went out and slammed the door.

Avis stood biting her lip hard, fighting back tears. There was a limit to what understanding could do and she had nearly reached it, but if Holt didn't need her his mother did, and she wouldn't give way to resentment or self-pity, however he behaved to her, she told herself. She drank what

was left of the coffee and forced herself to eat a
piece of toast.

The phone rang and it was Peter, Holt's brother,
ringing from Birmingham. Avis had spoken once
or twice to him on the phone since they had been
back in England. He sounded pleasant, she
thought, easy-going and much too nice for the
appalling Hazel.

She gave him the news about his mother. 'God,
that's bad!' He sounded really upset. 'What had I
better do? Should I come to London to see her?
It's a bit difficult just now—my wife's away, the
nanny's packed it in and I'm having a hell of a
time trying to get the kids looked after so that I
can get on with my job. But if you think I
should——'

Avis assured him that there was no point in his
doing anything this morning and promised to ring
him back as soon as there was any definite news,
and he seemed reassured. 'You sound like a trump,
Avis,' he told her. 'I can't wait to meet you. Old
Holt's found himself a treasure and no mistake!'

As she was replacing the receiver she heard the
front door of the flat open, and her heart missed a
beat. Had something bad happened, to bring Holt
back so soon?

Then a waft of expensive perfume reached her
and she turned round to see a woman standing in
the doorway. She was white-blonde, excessively
slim and her burgundy silk two-piece looked as if
it had been moulded to her body. She had a lovely,
sulky face that suggested hours spent with creams
and lotions. Not very young—she was probably
over thirty. Avis took all this in at a glance before
it dawned upon her that the woman must have a
key to the flat.

This must be Holt's current girl-friend, the one

that Hazel had been talking to on the phone at
Menton. Avis didn't know how she was so sure,
but she was.

The woman sauntered into the room, her eyes
travelling over Avis in the jeans and knitted top
she had pulled on early this morning when it
didn't seem to matter what she wore. 'So—you're
the new wife, are you?' Her lip curled contemptuously. 'I heard about you from Holt last night
and I thought I'd drop in and see what the dear
boy had landed himself with. Even more immature
than I'd imagined! I must introduce myself—
Leonie Hudson.' She held out a languid hand.

Avis ignored it. 'I don't think we have anything
to say to each other,' she said calmly. She wasn't
going to be intimidated by a woman out of Holt's
past—or out of his present, if that was the way it
was. She was his wife; she held the trump card. She
met the calculating greenish eyes without flinching.
'I'm very busy this morning, Miss—er—Hudson,
and I must ask you to leave.'

Surprise and fury registered for a moment on
the bored, insolent face. The painted lips curled
contemptuously. 'My, my, a vulgar little fishwife—
it's even worse than I thought! Poor Holt *has* had
to scrape the gutter to find himself a wife all in a
hurry. But never mind, he won't have to put up
with you for long. I expect you know all about
that, though.' Her eyes narrowed craftily. 'I
wonder how much he's paying you for being so
accommodating? I must ask him tonight. Goodbye,
my dear, I'm sure we won't meet again.'

She turned and lounged out of the room, and
Avis heard the front door close with a click. She
stood like a statue for a time, staring at nothing.
No need to wonder who the 'colleague' was! She
felt numb, as if nothing could surprise her or hurt

her any longer. Too much had happened too quickly. There was only one thing to concentrate upon, and that was Mrs Clavell, who liked her and needed her.

She tidied the flat, then she dressed in her brown office suit and went out into the King's Road. Here she bought milk and coffee and cheese and bread and carried them back to the flat. If Holt came home there would be something for him in the fridge. But she wouldn't be here, she would go to the hospital and stay there until she was no longer needed.

A week passed. Sometimes the hours dragged interminably, like the time that Avis sat frozen to ice in a warm waiting room, drinking cups of tea and trying not to picture what was going on in the operating theatre. Sometimes they flipped past almost unnoticed, as when she raced out to a launderette with Mrs Clavell's washing, her heart singing because she had just been told that her mother-in-law had come through the operation splendidly and the doctors were pleased and optimistic.

There were the times when she sat with Mrs Clavell and thought she saw a tinge of colour coming into the thin, pale cheeks; other times when Sister shooed Avis out of the room, her face grave because her patient was running a temperature. But as the days passed the line on the chart at the bottom of the bed steadied, and after that each day showed a slight improvement.

Avis devoted herself entirely to Mrs Clavell's needs sitting with her quietly for hours, when she needed to rest; reading to her or regaling her with bits of news from the papers; shopping for new nighties and toilet preparations; looking after her laundry; supplying her with books and magazines and keeping the flowers in her room fresh. She was a great favourite with all the nurses. Even Sister paid her the rare compliment of saying, 'Mrs Clavell is lucky to have such a devoted daughter-in-law.'

Holt came in every day at different times, according to the progress of his court case. Sometimes Avis was there when he came, and then she would disappear and leave them together. It was more than she could face—pretending to be a blissful new wife to Holt under his mother's eye. If they met in the hospital corridor they would stop and speak for a few minutes, about his mother's condition, or some detail connected with the flat—never about their relationship.

One day at the end of the first week she plucked up courage to ask him how the court case was getting on. 'So-so,' he said. He looked moody and bored, as if he wasn't concerned with it, or with her, and she didn't ask him again.

Avis had been keeping Peter, Holt's brother, informed by phone about his mother's condition, and on the third day after the operation he appeared at the hospital when Avis was sitting with Mrs Clavell. He wasn't a bit like Holt, she thought. He was just as tall but rather too heavy and his hair was fair and prematurely thinning. But she thought he was truly fond of his mother, and as he kissed her and held her hand and stood looking down into her face Avis thought there were tears in his eyes.

She left them together then, and later he took her out to a nearby café before he got his train back to Birmingham. He collected tea and cream cakes and sat back regarding Avis quizzically out of world-weary eyes. 'So,' he said, taking a bite of cake and pushing the plate away with a grimace, 'you married old Holt, did you? Out of the blue, wasn't it? Trust Holt to leave it until the eleventh hour—or what he thought was the eleventh hour. How long have you been together— I've rather lost touch with Holt's activities since we've been up in Birmingham.'

Avis took a sip of weak tea. 'We—haven't been together,' she said. 'We only met each other about three weeks ago.' Then, greatly daring because she hardly knew Peter, but she couldn't stop the question blurting out, 'What do you mean by "eleventh hour"? Please tell me—there seems to be some mystery that I don't know about. Your wife said something that I didn't understand when I saw her in Menton.'

He looked at her curiously. 'So you encountered Hazel, did you? And how did you get on?'

Avis flushed crimson and said nothing, and he grinned crookedly. 'Yes, I thought as much—you needn't tell me. It was a facer for her, hearing you'd married Holt, was that it?'

Avis nodded. 'She seemed—upset about it.'

Peter jerked back his head and roared with laughter. 'Upset? I bet she was upset! My lady wife has been fancying herself as mistress of Dell Cottage when my mother passes on. Have you been there—it isn't really a cottage, you know, it's the Big House of the village. Hazel fancies the idea of being the lady of the manor—handing out goodies to the peasants, organising the W.I., bossing the Mothers' Union, all that sort of thing. Nobody ever dreamed that Holt would get married, he was always dead against it.' He grinned with relish. 'Golly, that's one in the eye for Hazel!'

He glanced across the table at Avis's troubled

face and added, 'As you may have gathered, my
wife and I are—rather less than devoted to each
other. In fact, we're all washed up, and this will
just about add the finishing touch to our unhappy
union.' He grimaced sourly. 'Hazel won't have
anything to gain now by staying with me. I'll be
able to go ahead with a divorce. I have you to
thank for that relief, Avis.'

'*Me?*' Avis said faintly. 'I—don't understand.
Tell me in words of one syllable, please, Peter.'

He looked oddly at her. 'Holt didn't tell you? I
thought—oh well, never mind. It's quite simple
really. My father inherited Dell Cottage from his
father, who took it over from his father—my
great-grandfather. In those days it was just an
ordinary cottage, but my great-grandfather made a
lot of money in the wool business—which was still
thriving in the Cotswolds—and started to tart
the place up. The original cottage is very old and
it's been added to over the years. Very picturesque
and countryfied if you like that sort of thing. I
must confess I prefer the bright lights of the city
myself.'

'Go on,' said Avis, unconscious that her hands
were gripping the edge of the table.

'Are you O.K.? You look very pale. I'm not sure
I should be telling you all this.' The dissipated blue
eyes looked slightly guilty. 'You know, Holt will
slay me if——'

'*Please* go on,' Avis said tightly.

He shrugged. 'Well, there isn't much more
really. My father had a passion for the old house,
he was nuts about it and after he retired he made it
a sort of shrine, a monument to *his* father and
grandfather. He was what you'd have called one of
the old school, I suppose. Handing down from
father to son—that sort of lark—meant a lot to

him. It must have been a terrible blow to him that Holt—the eldest son—didn't seem hooked on the idea of marrying—quite the reverse in fact, he was always running down the state of nuptial bliss.' Peter pulled a wry face. 'I guess he had something there. I married at twenty myself—a terrible mistake. But Holt was the cautious one, I expect because of his legal training, and he managed to avoid the tender trap.' He looked at Avis and his fleshy cheeks went rather red. 'Until now, I mean.'

Very quietly Avis said, 'And why did he have to get married now—in such a hurry? To a girl he's only known a week? Why does your wife think he was being pressured in some way?'

Peter broke the remains of his cake into small crumbs and sat looking down at them. 'Well——' he mumbled at last, 'I suppose it's because my dear wife always thinks the worst—jumps to the obvious conclusion. And, of course, we've always known about my father's will.'

'Ah!' breathed Avis. It was like one of those horror films where the sides of the wall close in on you, hideously and inevitably. She felt as if life was already being crushed out of her.

'My father, I suppose, did the only thing he could do as he was so hooked on the idea of the family estate being handed down through the generations. He left everything to my mother during her lifetime, but on her death Dell Cottage was to go to Holt—*if* he was married by then. If not, it would come to me. I was already married, you see, with two lusty male offspring to carry on the family line. Limbs of Satan they are, too!' he grimaced.

'I never gave the house a lot of thought,' he went on. 'For one thing I didn't fancy living in the country and being one of the landed gentry. For another, it didn't seem an urgent matter. Mama is only just over fifty and—although I know she's been a bit—what's the word?—delicate, I suppose I thought it was the ones who had little ailments that lived to be a hundred. Holt thought so too,' he added glumly.

'I see.' Suddenly Avis felt very calm. 'And then he found that she wasn't going to live to be a hundred—in fact, that she might not survive an operation? So—in order to be sure of his inheritance he had to be on the safe side and get married all in a hurry.'

But why me? she thought dully. Why not the Leonie woman? Then she remembered Hazel's words on the phone to Leonie: 'What a tragedy your divorce is so long in coming through.' It all began to fit in perfectly, like some diabolical Chinese puzzle.

Peter lifted his head and looked at her and his blue eyes were curiously gentle. 'Is that how it looks to you?'

'Well——' she spread out her hands helplessly, 'doesn't it look like that to you?'

'Oh, I don't know,' he said, taking hold of her hand and patting it, while he watched her face anxiously. 'There might be some other explanation.'

Avis stared back at him, her huge brown eyes clouded. Then slowly tears gathered and trickled down her cheeks and she lowered her head, covering her face with her hands.

Peter looked round the crowded tea-room, faintly embarrassed. He leaned forward and murmured, 'Don't cry, little one, it may not be as bad as you think.'

Through her sobs he caught the words that forced themselves haltingly from her. 'He—he said he loved me,' Avis mourned.

That seemed the worst thing of all.

CHAPTER EIGHT

In the days that followed Avis wondered how you could go on living an apparently normal life when three-quarters of you was dead. She kept thinking of that old song: 'My feet could step and walk, my lips could move and talk, and yet my heart stood still.' Her heart wasn't standing still now, it felt as if it had stopped altogether.

The days were busy, but at night there was nothing to do but lie awake in the big bed at Holt's flat and think. Round and round her thoughts went like buzzing insects, until she could lie still no longer and had to get up and switch on all the lights and pace around the flat, her bare toes sinking into the plushy carpet.

She went over and over everything that had happened and it all fitted so well, so horribly well. Holt hadn't believed that his mother was really ill, not until the last minute. If he ever thought about it he must have told himself that he had plenty of time to find a wife, years and years. And then suddenly he had found that he might not have any time at all. He wasn't happy-go-lucky like Peter; he would feel a sense of obligation to his father's wishes, to his role as eldest son, inheriting the family estate and handing it on to *his* son. Her mouth softened at the thought of bearing Holt's son. What heaven it would have been if he had meant what he said—if he had really loved her!

How long before he came to her with the truth and said he wanted an annulment of their marriage? It had served its purpose. *She* had served her purpose. Mrs Clavell was getting better every day now and Doctor Trimley had assured her that the condition had been spotted in time and had promised her a complete recovery and many years of active life ahead of her.

Holt's legal battle was still going on. He had brought fresh evidence into court and when Avis read the reports in the paper to Mrs Clavell it looked as if he might win his case for the defence. In spite of the hours of work that he had found it necessary to put in, Avis hadn't really realised that it was such a very important case, but for two days running now it hit the national headlines. His mother wanted to hear every word that was printed about the case and hundreds of words were printed.

Holt's principal in the law firm called one day to see Mrs Clavell and left her in a state of euphoria. 'My dear,' she told Avis, 'it looks as if we have a genius in the family. I wish you could have heard Mr Denvers. He doesn't usually hand out bouquets but he told me that Holt's handling of the case was brilliant. Brilliant—that was the very word he used.' Her eyes glowed with pride. 'I think from what he hinted that Holt will be offered a partnership in the firm very soon, isn't that wonderful?'

'Wonderful,' echoed Avis dutifully.

One afternoon Avis went to see Mr Hanworthy, and found him free and delighted to see her. 'Sit down, Avis, and tell me all your news. How is your mother-in-law? I was sorry to hear about her illness.'

Avis told him that Mrs Clavell was making a good recovery. 'But I felt guilty about leaving you in the lurch so suddenly, Mr Hanworthy.'

'Not to worry,' he said, patting her hand in a

fatherly way. 'Your husband explained it all. I've taken Cynthia on in your place and she's shaping up quite well.'

'And how is that clever young husband of yours? I've been following his progress in the Williamson case. Following it with some admiration, I may tell you.' He beamed at her. 'A highly complex brief—he seems to be handling it admirably. You've got yourself a rising star, Avis. I can see you as wife of a High Court Judge, all in due time.'

There was a tap on the door and Cynthia came in to say his next appointment had arrived so Avis was spared the need to think of something to say in reply.

She stood up and said goodbye. Mr Hanworthy pressed her hand. 'Goodbye, my dear.' He chuckled. 'Let me know if you want your old job back.'

Avis could still hear him chuckling at his own little joke as she left his office and went out to say goodbye to the rest of the staff. She wouldn't be asking for her old job back, when her marriage was over. That part of her life was finished. For the first time she wondered what she would do when she was alone again, and the answer presented itself immediately.

Tears stung behind her eyes as she walked to the station to get a train back into town. She had tried standing on her own two feet and had failed miserably. Like a little girl, desperately hurt, she needed her mother.

At last came the day when Mrs Clavell was allowed to leave hospital. It had been arranged that she should go home to the Cotswolds to convalesce.

'I've made all the necessary arrangements,' Holt

told Avis as they met outside his mother's room.
'I'll drive you both, and the nurse, to Dell Cottage
myself as soon as court rises. I'll have to get back
to town almost straight away though.'

'Yes, of course,' Avis said tonelessly. Back to
Leonie, of course.

He shot her a quick look. 'What's the matter,
Avis? Are you getting too tired? Has all this been
too much for you?' He sounded more impatient
than concerned, she thought. 'There won't be too
much for you to do when you get there. Nurse
Clayton will stay on as long as she's needed. And
Mrs Bolton is what they call a treasure of a
housekeeper,' he added. 'You'll like her.'

Why should he say that? Was he expecting her
to stay for any length of time at Dell Cottage? A
tiny ray of hope touched Avis. 'How long shall I
be staying there?' she asked casually, just as a wife
would, making plans with her husband to suit
them both.

His eyes fixed on her for a moment. 'Oh, for as
long as Mama needs you, I suppose,' he said.
'You'll be happy there, it's a lovely spot.'

She almost burst out, How do you think I could
be happy, with everything so horribly wrong
between us? but Holt looked at his watch and said,
'I must go. I've got to be back in court.' He was
miles away from her again. 'Can you cope?' he
added almost as an afterthought. 'What a
question—of course you can cope. You've been
splendid all through this, Avis.'

She watched him stride away down the long
hospital corridor, and her heart seemed to squeeze
up inside her as her eyes followed the tall straight
form, the broad shoulders under their immacu-
lately-fitting jacket, the thick dark hair where once
her fingers had curled in ecstasy. As he passed out

of sight she swallowed a sob. Splendid! A word of praise he might use to an efficient secretary. If he had loved her he would have given her a quick hug then and there and whispered, 'You've been wonderful, darling.'

Her eyes misted. It seemed a long time since he had spoken lovingly to her, and she didn't suppose he ever would again. There would be no need to pretend any longer. He was married, he had complied with the terms of his father's will, that was all he had ever wanted from her. Not that it would matter now; his mother wasn't going to die, not for a long, long time. He must regret bitterly that he had rushed into marriage. But if he had gone into it hastily, she supposed he could get out of it just as hastily. Hazel's words came back to her, cutting into her like thin sharp blades: 'I don't suppose he's had sex with you since he married you, has he? No, I thought not. He's a clever bastard, he knows all the legal angles.'

Avis knew the legal angles too, she hadn't worked for a solicitor for nothing. There were ways of voiding a marriage that hadn't been 'consummated'—she winced away from the word. One day soon, she supposed, when Holt was less tied up with his court case, he would come to her and ask for his freedom. She tried to imagine what he would say to her. That he had acted too hastily, been carried away by his mother's wishes, had been piqued because she had run away from him?

Oh God, it was all such a mess! Dispiritedly, Avis turned and went back into Mrs Clavell's room, fixing a bright smile on her lips.

They drove to the Cotswolds two days later. Holt had been held up with an interview and it was almost dark by the time they finally drew up outside a studded oak door with a welcoming light above it. The house itself was no more than a grey hulk against a bank of high trees, but even though she couldn't see it properly Avis was immediately conscious of the feeling of peace here. There were blackbirds singing in the dusk and the smell of damp grass and spring flowers.

Holt helped his mother from the car and she leaned on his arm and sniffed the air. 'Heaven!' she sighed. 'I shall be weeding in the garden in no time at all.'

But as soon as they got into the house Nurse Clayton, an amiable young woman with a voice that spoke in the tones of authority, insisted that her patient should go straight to bed.

'You'll come up and see me, both of you?' Mrs Clavell looked towards Avis, then to Holt, who was carrying the luggage in from the car. 'Do you really have to go back to town tonight, Holt dear?'

He dumped a suitcase at the foot of the stairs. ' 'Fraid so, Mama. Duty calls.' He smiled at her. 'But when this case is over I promise to invite myself for as long as you'll have me.'

'And you won't mind leaving your new wife with me until then?' She grimaced towards Avis and added, 'The penalty of marrying a barrister, my dear!'

Holt put an arm round Avis's shoulder and she almost flinched away because his touch was agony, like holding a frozen hand to the fire. 'I expect she'll make herself useful,' he smiled. 'She's a very useful young lady, as I'm sure you agree, Mama.'

How could he joke like that, just as if everything was normal? She turned away, biting her lip as he followed his mother and the nurse upstairs.

Mrs Bolton, the housekeeper, had been waiting in the hall to greet them and then had retired to the background. But now she came forward to Avis, beaming. 'It's a pleasure to have you here, Mrs Clavell, and may I please offer my very best wishes. It's been a worrying time, what with the mistress being so ill, but it's all turned out for the best now.' Having delivered her little speech she smoothed down her greying hair, which was already fixed into a neat bun on top of her head, and suggested that Avis might like to see her bedroom.

She led the way up an oak staircase, along a passage and into a large, attractively-furnished bedroom with an electric fire glowing to supplement the heating. 'It's chilly these evenings,' Mrs Bolton chattered on about the weather. 'I hope you and the young master will be comfortable in here, Mrs Clavell. I put you here in the guest room, but of course you will be able to choose another room later on, if you wish.' She pulled back the long coral-pink curtains. 'Ah, it's too dark to see the garden now, but it's a real picture, I can tell you. I hope you'll be very happy here, Mrs Clavell.' She closed the curtains again.

Avis heard herself saying the right things; she could hardly tell the housekeeper that she wouldn't be staying very long, and that when she left she wouldn't be coming back. She was thankful when Mrs Bolton said that she must go down and see to the supper, and she was alone. She unpacked her case slowly, setting her toilet things out on the polished walnut dressing table with the lace mats, avoiding looking at her face in the big triple mirror, in case she was horrified at what she saw there. She hung up the few clothes she had brought with her, and every time she passed the big double bed in the middle of the room she closed her eyes. She would not be sharing it with her husband, she knew that with a deadly sick certainty.

She turned quickly as Holt came into the room. He paused beside a writing table, picked up a magazine and put it down again. 'I ought to get back to London straight away,' he said, 'but Mrs Bolton has got supper ready for us and I don't want to hurt her feelings, she's a good soul.' He glanced towards the bed. 'You'll be comfortable here?'

'Of course,' Avis said stiffly. 'It's a beautiful room. Shall we go down to supper, then?' She swept past him and along the passage.

Nurse Clayton joined them for supper, set at one end of a long table in the oak-panelled dining room. She was a bright, cheerful soul and asked bright, cheerful questions about everything—the house, the garden, the neighbourhood. If she noticed that Holt's replies were monosyllabic and that Avis hardly spoke at all she was too good and tactful a nurse to show any surprise, but as soon as supper was over she excused herself to go up and see to her patient.

Alone with Holt, Avis found that her mouth was dry and it was impossible to think of anything to say. Holt would be driving back to town immediately, she supposed, and it would be easier for both of them if they didn't have to talk to each other. Tonight wasn't the time.

So now, without a word to him, she got up and followed the nurse out of the room, and went upstairs to the bedroom. She didn't suppose Holt would follow, but she sat tense and shivering in the chair beside the electric fire for some time, just in case he did.

A few minutes later she heard the noise of a car outside in the drive. He had left—left without a word to her. Numbly she got up and took off her travelling suit and pulled on a fleecy white angora wrap. Her mother had given it to her as a Christmas present just before she left for Australia, and Avis had brought it with her—it seemed somehow comforting, as if to remind her that there was someone who loved her.

Then she peeped in to Mrs Clavell's room, but Nurse Jackson put a finger to her lips as she came to the door. 'She's sleeping,' she whispered. 'The journey's been tiring for her, that's all, but she'll be fine in the morning.'

Avis went back to her own room—the room that had been prepared for herself and Holt. Mrs Bolton had evidently found his brushes and toilet things in the room he usually occupied and had transferred them to the dressing table here. Avis picked up a bottle of cologne and sniffed it absently and immediately Holt seemed to be there beside her, his arms around her, so potent was the memory that the smell of the cologne brought back to her. Tears gathered thickly in her eyes and the bottle dropped with a clatter from her fingers. At the same moment Holt himself opened the door and came into the room.

'I thought you'd gone,' she said tonelessly, not looking at him. 'I heard a car.'

He came towards her as she stood by the dressing table. 'That was probably Bolton coming in. He has a job in Stroud three days a week.'

'Are you leaving, then? Your mother is asleep, I've just been in to see.'

In the mirror she saw him nod. 'Yes, I've been too. She looks very peaceful. It will be a real tonic to her to be back here, she loves the place so much. The doctor seemed to think that it would be good for her to be here instead of going to a convalescent home somewhere.'

'Yes,' said Avis. She wondered why he was lingering to tell her this. They had been over it all before.

She had gathered herself together sufficiently now to turn and face him, and she was shocked by his expression. He looked as if he hadn't slept for days, the thin, clever face was haggard and the dark, hooded eyes were deeply shadowed.

Impulsively she put a hand out and touched his arm. 'Don't worry any more, Holt,' she said, 'it's all over now and she's going to be all right.'

He nodded. 'I know. It's not Mama that——' He wrenched himself away. 'Oh hell,' he muttered.

He was going now. Avis's eyes were fixed on his back. The palms of her hands were sweating and her heart was beating suffocatingly, but she knew that somehow she must find the courage to do the most difficult thing she had ever done in her life.

She ran after him and put her hand on his arm. 'Do you have to go back tonight?' she said, her voice shaking. She reached up and put her arms round his neck and pressed her cheek against his cold hard cheek. 'Won't you stay with me, my darling? I want you—I love you so much.'

There was a ghastly silence. Oh God, she thought, I shouldn't have said that, it's only brought the end nearer. He'll tell me now. She tensed her stomach as if against a blow.

Very gently Holt disengaged himself and put her arms down beside her. Then he moved away. 'I've hurt you badly, Avis,' he said woodenly, 'and that's not the least of my crimes.' Through her tears she saw the tormented look on his face. 'I'm sorry—sorry about everything.'

She sank down on to the bed, leaning forward, cramming her fist against her mouth like a child.

From a long way away she heard him say, 'I'd better go now.'

She didn't see him go out of the room, but through her sobs she heard the door close behind him, then the sound of his car driving away.

After a long time she looked at her watch. It was half-past ten. It would be early morning in Australia. Moving like an automaton, she reached out and drew the telephone towards her, fumbling in her handbag for her diary with her mother's number written in it. Her hands were icy cold as she dialled the international code. At one point her finger slipped and she had to replace the receiver and start again. But at last she got it right and sat waiting for a reply, yearning to hear her mother's dear, familiar voice.

She wasn't conscious of the door opening or the footsteps on the thick carpet. An arm came from behind her, took the receiver out of her hand and replaced it on its cradle.

She spun round with a choky cry to see Holt towering above her. 'Who were you phoning?' he demanded.

She got to her feet. If he had come back for explanations then he could hear hers. 'My mother, in Adelaide,' she said, and was amazed how calm her voice sounded. 'I plan to fly out there and join her. I won't need to ask you for the fare, I have enough saved up of my own. It will be more convenient if I'm out of the way, you'll have a stronger case for annulment. If you like you can say I refuse to—to—what do they call it?—to consummate the marriage. I don't much care.'

He gripped her by her two arms, staring into her face, his own face ashen-white.

'What the bloody hell are you talking about?' he demanded violently.

'I think you know perfectly well.'

He shook her until her teeth rattled. 'I don't know. Come on, tell me.'

Her eyes widened, glazed. 'Don't you want an annulment of our marriage? It wasn't necessary to marry me after all, was it, now that your mother is getting better?'

Holt sank down on to the bed and pulled her down beside him. 'Avis,' he said, more quietly now, 'you seem to be talking utter rubbish. Suppose you just tell me quietly what all this is about. What is this extraordinary story you've cooked up?'

'*I've* cooked up?' she cried indignantly. 'I haven't cooked anything up! I've heard it all from your relatives—what you didn't think fit to tell me yourself. That under the terms of your father's will you had to be married at the time of your mother's death, in order to inherit the property here. And that when you knew she had to have this operation and her life might be in danger it was necessary for you to get a wife urgently. I was handy, so you asked me.'

He pushed back his hair with a little groan of disbelief. 'Just a minute, who told you all this?'

'Well—your brother's wife, Hazel, told me, when I saw her in Menton. She said you'd obviously married me so quickly as a—as a convenience, and that you'd want to end the marriage as soon as you could. She said that you wouldn't—wouldn't sleep with me because you could get an annulment more easily if you didn't.'

'And you believed her?' said Holt through narrowed lips. 'That bitch?'

'No, I didn't. I told her she was lying, that you married me because you loved me, and she laughed in my face and said you were living with some woman called Leonie, but she was married already. I was going to tell you when I got back to England. I wanted to hear you deny it, laugh it away, but—but I couldn't get near you, you seemed to have shut yourself off from me.' The words were coming in a flood now. 'Then, later on, when I met your brother Peter he said something about your father's will and I asked him to explain. I still couldn't believe it. I told myself you were busy, you were worried, that it would all come right.'

She gulped and was silent.

'Go on,' Holt said very quietly.

She turned her head away. 'Then—tonight—when you rejected me, it all came together and I—I had to believe it,' she said very low. 'I thought you hated me, that you didn't want me.'

He groaned. 'Hated *you*? My darling girl it was myself I hated, I've been an utter bastard to you lately, but when you hate yourself the whole world is twisted out of shape. And want you? God, if you knew how I've wanted you! But I was in the blackest of black guilty hells. I knew that if I'd been more sensitive, more perceptive, more—loving, I'd have realised ages ago that Mama was really ill, that she was heading up for a crisis. The thought kept tormenting me that if she died I was to blame. I couldn't forgive myself.'

He ran a hand desperately through his dark hair. 'I felt like mud. I suppose I was punishing myself, but don't you see I *couldn't* just go on grabbing my own happiness, just as if nothing had happened. But God knows how much I was tempted.' He groaned. 'Oh, darling, when you said you loved me tonight I think I knew how a man must feel when he walks out of prison into the sunlight! I began to feel—cleansed. You'll never know what it meant to me to hear you say that. I'd nearly reached the motorway when it finally hit me and I had to come back to you.'

His arms went round her and he pushed her gently down on to the bed and stroked her hair away from her face, looking down into her eyes. 'I adore you, my love,' he said brokenly. 'You're everything I've ever dreamed of and I want you with me always—for the rest of our lives. I'll be awkward and hard to live with sometimes, when I get a difficult case. Will you be able to put up with me?'

For answer she reached up and drew his head down and he started to rub his cheek soothingly against hers. She began to feel a warm tide rising inside her, seeping into every corner of her body, thawing the ice of the last days.

'Can you stay with me for a little while?' she whispered. 'I don't want to be alone again.' Her hand crept inside his thin shirt, her fingers tracing the warm smooth skin of his shoulder, the growth of hair that ran down between his ribs.

'Try to stop me,' he muttered. She felt him shudder and then he was pulling off his clothes and tossing them to the floor. In the shaded light from the bedside lamp he undressed her slowly, his eyes feasting on her smooth softness, pale against the darker pink of the coverlet. When the last filmy garment had gone he still gazed down at her, as if he couldn't believe that this was happening. Then with a groan, he was on her, his mouth taking hers thirstily. Her lips parted to him, her body moving against his in a mounting need as desire licked her like a flame. His hands stroked her thighs and moved down to awake shattering new sensations that made her moan aloud. All the misery of the last days was dissolved in a throbbing, delirious tide of passion as their two bodies clung and fused together.

Holt whispered brokenly, 'Darling—darling—I love you so—love you—love you——' and she responded with little, inarticulate cries of longing until soon the rising tide of ecstasy reached its height. Through the thudding in her ears she heard Holt's own cry of fulfilment and for a long moment they clung together speechless and transported, and then slowly, blissfully, they relaxed, hearts pounding against each other, until gradually they lay still and quiet and utterly fulfilled, their arms about each other.

At some time in the night Avis wakened and stretched out her hand in the darkness. When it encountered nothing she let out a little scream. 'Holt—where are you?'

A warm strong hand found hers, pressed it. 'Here, my love, trying to dress in the dark.' He switched on the bedside lamp. 'That's better, now I needn't put my socks on inside out. It might give a wrong impression in court!' He was laughing, he sounded quite different, full of vitality and confidence. She had never heard his voice quite like this.

'W-what time is it?' She pulled herself up sleepily.

'Time for me to go,' he said. 'Don't wake up, my love, sleep and dream of me, and I'll be back at the very first moment.'

The light went out again and through a haze of sleep she felt him bend over her and gather her warmth tenderly for a moment into his arms. Then the door closed softly behind him, and with a sigh of content she drifted off to sleep again. He would come back; he loved her; that was all she wanted.

'In the big fraud trial at the Old Bailey the jury is still considering its verdict——'

That had been the news at one o'clock, since when Avis wouldn't allow herself to switch the radio on again. She wanted to hear the result from Holt himself. If he had won she would rejoice with him and if he had lost perhaps she could console him just a little.

It had been a strange day—tranquil on the surface and bubbling with joy beneath. Much of the time Avis had spent with Mrs Clavell, who was fretting at having to stay in bed, on Nurse Clayton's orders, to recuperate from yesterday's journey.

'I feel ready to get up a little,' she had insisted. 'In fact I feel better than I have done for ages and ages.'

'Patience!' the nurse had smiled. 'Tomorrow, perhaps.' And Mrs Clavell had to agree. 'But I can hardly wait to see my beloved Dell Cottage from the outside, then I shall know I'm really home. You do like it, don't you, Avis?'

'I think it's the most beautiful house I've ever seen,' Avis said quite sincerely, and indeed she had fallen in love with the low, rambling Cotswold stone house with its passages opening out into gracious rooms, its flights of stairs tucked away in unexpected places, its window-seats and inglenooks and weathered black ceiling beams.

Now it was nearly seven o'clock and court must have risen hours ago, but still Holt hadn't come home. Until she had seen him again she couldn't let herself believe that last night had really happened.

She waited for him in the long drawing-room. 'This is Mrs Clavell's favourite room,' Mrs Bolton had told her this morning, when she took her on a tour round the house, and Avis had agreed that it was indeed a beautiful room, with its mellow, lovingly-polished old furniture and deep chintz-covered chairs and sofas. She had been in the garden earlier, and picked masses of daffodils to arrange in jugs and pots around the room, and now the spring fragrance filled the air, along with the scent of the apple logs burning in the great fire-basket.

Avis wandered restlessly about the room, glancing at the watercolours on the walls, at the photographs that stood in silver frames on the wide shelf over the inglenook fireplace. There was one of Peter and Hazel as bride and bridegroom, Hazel with a smug expression on her thin, colourless face that even a flowing veil could not conceal. Another of two boys of about three and five, with thick, pouting lips and Hazel's pale, malicious eyes. Some small boys could be fairly nasty creatures, and Avis couldn't help smiling as she remembered their grandmother shuddering, 'Little horrors!' Looking at the two of them, she wondered just what they had done to earn their grandmother's disapproval.

There was a photograph of Holt, aloof and impressive in wig and gown. She stood a long time in front of that one, staring into the dark, magnetic eyes, trying to hear him say, 'I love you,' but it was impossible.

'Not very flattering, is it?' His voice from the doorway made her spin round, her heart leaping. He stood there smiling at her and with a little cry she flew across the room into his arms, to be held there tightly, her head pressed against his shoulder.

Then he kissed her until she could hardly breathe. When he finally took his mouth away it was to say, deadpan, 'Well—we won.'

'Holt—darling, darling, darling! Oh, how absolutely wonderful, you're marvellous!'

'That's what I like to hear,' he grinned. 'Come and sit down and tell me again.' He drew her towards the deep sofa in front of the fire.

'I've been up to see Mama,' he said, 'she seems to be getting along splendidly.' He stared into the glowing logs and his face was sober. 'I've got off far easier than I deserve.'

'Oh, *please*,' Avis begged, 'you mustn't go on blaming yourself. She wouldn't want it.'

'And you've forgiven me for being such a brute to you?'

'Were you?' she said dreamily.

Holt drew her closer. 'I seem to remember our wedding night, when I had to work into the small hours and creep into our nuptial bed, dead to the world and afraid to wake my wife up.'

'I wasn't asleep,' Avis admitted. 'But I knew how utterly exhausted you were. It wasn't until I got to Menton and Hazel said her piece that I began to—to wonder a bit. And then when you said you weren't coming home at night while the trial lasted I did get a bit worried, I must admit.'

He groaned. 'By that time I'd worked myself up into a real state. I wanted you desperately, but I wouldn't allow myself to have what I longed for. Must be my Puritan ancestors!' He gave a hollow laugh. 'I daren't let myself get too near you, so I took a room at a hotel, to be out of the sight and sound of you. Can you understand?'

'I—I think so,' Avis whispered. 'I thought you were going to—to Leonie on those nights.'

'Leonie?' His head jerked up. 'I suppose that was another of Hazel's little poison darts?'

'I heard Hazel talking to her on the phone, telling her that you'd married a——' She stopped, her cheeks flushing scarlet as she remembered the humiliation of that moment. 'And then Leonie herself came to the flat one day when you were out. She was—rather horrid.'

'I can imagine,' he said darkly. He laid his mouth against her hair. 'Poor sweet, I really let you in for it, didn't I? I've been so bloody selfish.

'And anyway,' he went on, 'Leonie and I were finished months ago, although she wouldn't accept it. She was separated from her husband and when she started talking about getting a divorce I could see the way the wind was blowing. But it was over for me before that—a little of Leonie goes a long, long way. Incidentally, it was Hazel who pushed her on to me in the first place—it suited Hazel's game only too well, of course, to have me involved with a married woman.' He smiled bitterly. 'So long as I wasn't married there was a chance of Peter inheriting Dell Cottage and all that goes with it—and that was Hazel's great ambition.'

Avis nodded slowly. 'Peter told me. He said their marriage was on the rocks, and that this would finish it. I—I think he's rather pleased.'

Holt said, 'It would be the best thing that could happen for Peter. That woman's a menace, he should never have married her. The awful example of his plight was one of the things that made me look askance at marriage for myself. All of which goes to show——' he smoothed back her hair and kissed her temple softly '—what fools these mortals be, in the words of Puck!'

'And do you still think that Mama invited me to Menton to trap you?' she asked demurely, her sherry-brown eyes glinting.

His finger traced a line from her forehead down to her mouth and he kissed her softly. 'I'm willing to bet she did. As soon as she saw you she must have thought to herself, "This is the right girl to tempt old Holt into marriage." And she was dead right. But don't let's talk about that now, let's talk about us.' He glanced at the gilt carriage-clock on the mantelshelf. 'Three quarters of an hour before Mrs Bolton brings on the food,' he said. 'I suggest that we put a call through to your mother—will it be too early in the morning for her?'

'She won't mind being wakened up to hear good news,' Avis said happily.

'It's even better news than you think, sweetheart. My chief is so chuffed with winning this case that he's suggested I've earned a month's leave, for a honeymoon. What do you say if we fly out to Adelaide?'

'Oh,' Avis gasped, 'that would be heaven! Let's go and ring her straight away.' She jumped to her feet.

'*Almost* straight away,' Holt amended. 'I suggest we go up to the bedroom to phone, it's so comfy up there. But before we put the call through I have something else in mind for us.' His arm circled her slender waist and he drew her close. 'Can you guess what it is?'

She looked up into the thin, clever face and wondered how she could ever have thought him cold and remote. There was such a blaze of love and tenderness in the dark eyes that the heat rose into her cheeks and she lowered her head in sudden shyness.

'Is there a prize for the right answer?' she whispered, and his laugh was a shout of triumph as he led her to the foot of the stairs.

'You bet there is,' he said. 'For both of us.'